SHADO

C000136989

BARB

A Legend Will Rise

SHADOW OF THE
BARBARIAN
A Legend Will Rise

Two Titanic Tales from a Lost Age

BY
JOHN THANE

DCO BOOKS

Shadow of the Barbarian
Copyright © John Thane, 2017
First Published 2017
DCO Books

This edition published 2018
by Proglen Trading Co., Ltd.
Bangkok Thailand
http://www.dco.co.th

ISBN 978-1790947522

For the leopard women of Bioko Island, the exiled Russian Princesses of Samarkand and the apple blossom sing-song girls of Nanjing. Bless 'em all.

Shadow of the Barbarian
by John Thane

CONTENTS

INTRODUCTION

Thirteen thousand years ago, human civilization flourished across the face of the Earth, until a blazing asteroid plunged out of the firmament and struck with the force of several thousand nuclear bombs exploding simultaneously. This cataclysmic event triggered a sudden and shocking climate change, ushering in an ice age that swept the planet for over fifteen hundred years. In order to survive, humankind reverted to becoming hunter-gatherers, degenerating into savagery before beginning the upward climb toward civilization again.

The elder civilizations were lost to history, remembered only in myths and legends.

Until now …

SHADOW OF THE BARBARIAN

3

ONE

The Emperor's sea-palace sprawled along the shoreline, its white marbled magnificence pulsating in the hot sun, like the bleached bones of some long dead sea leviathan. In the cool shadows of a deep terrace, Princess Semoon stretched like a lazy cat and raised dark liquid eyes to survey the green, sparkling ocean. Shading those eyes with one graceful hand, she could discern a series of dark smudges on the ocean's far horizon. As she watched, a light stabbed from one of them. Quickly she turned her head to observe the excitement this flickering signal generated amongst the men who were gathered along the terrace. Three royal signalers conferred, came swiftly to an agreement, and then scampered, as one, over to an expectant knot of splendidly armored Admirals. They huddled together briefly, before the Admirals broke away to stride importantly toward a crowd of richly attired noblemen. The noblemen parted to reveal a young, vigorous figure standing, gazing into an ornamental pool. The man turned at the Admirals' approach and, though dressed in only a simple tunic, he dominated the gathering of noblemen with his presence.

"Sire, the flagship of the notorious pirate, Ben-Alzur, has been fired and sunk," one of the Admirals announced grandly. "There were no prisoners taken."

The Emperor's wide grin shone briefly upon them all before he spun about and clicked his fingers. Instantly, fleets of miniature war-galleys, propelled by hidden strings, stirred the placid waters of the pool. The nobles gathered at the pool's edge, their faces rapt. When Ben-Alzur's tiny flagship ignited on cue, a polite ripple of applause floated down the long terrace.

Princess Semoon yawned. Men, they were such boys. Even her brother, the Emperor, was a child in her eyes. She

5

became aware of Tarok, her bodyguard, eyeing her hungrily. Her gaze lingered over his huge, muscled frame. Well, she thought, maybe they were not all children. Turning back to the ocean, her brow wrinkled. There were fingers gripping the edge of the terrace's gilded balustrade. She gave a small involuntary cry when a muscular, sun-bronzed arm flung itself over the rail. Then a head appeared. A pair of startling green eyes regarded her levelly for a moment, before their owner sprang nimbly onto the terrace. Naked but for a twist of loincloth, he strode toward her, leaving a seawater trail across the marble paving. Without pausing, he snatched a flagon of wine from a side table and began pouring it down his throat.

She arched one sardonic eyebrow. "That's a fine Arcturian red. It can only be appreciated if sipped."

He threw down the empty flagon and belched. "I appreciated it alright. That salt water dried me out. Hell of a swim!" Looking down at her, he suddenly grinned, displaying strong white teeth against bronzed skin.

She found herself grinning back at him.

"Aren't you afraid, girl?" he asked.

She gave him a look of cool regard. "Why should I be? I am a Princess, and you are a dead pirate," she answered calmly, indicating the pack of guardsmen rushing toward them with bared steel in their fists.

"You have a point," he conceded. With a sudden swoop, he grabbed the divan she lay upon and tipped her unceremoniously onto the floor. Holding the divan before him like a battering ram, he charged into the guardsmen. Two of the men went down. The others found themselves pinned between the balustrade and the heavy piece of furniture, which the intruder held like a shield. Try as they might, they could not reach him with their blades.

The Princess lay in an undignified heap. For a few moments, she was too stunned to move. Lifting her head, she blew an errant lock of raven hair from her face and, despite herself, shouted out a warning.

The pirate must have heard her because he ducked to one side, just as Tarok's blade sliced toward him. Twisting away, he leapt forward and slid across the slick marble floor on his belly, toward a fallen saber. Grabbing the saber, he rolled to his feet and waited. The guardsmen disentangled themselves from the divan and, led by Tarok, advanced.

Semoon was delighted to feel her heart beating wildly in her chest. She almost clapped her hands with excitement. Taking the opportunity, she studied the intruder. He was very tall and wide across the shoulders, though not as massive as Tarok. She noted the great coils of twisted muscle and taut sinew that ridged his scarred brown hide. Despite the tangle of dripping black hair that hung about his face, she could see he was grinning. His features, she thought, were brutal, though handsome.

When Tarok saw the Emperor and his retinue approaching, he motioned for the guardsmen to stand back. He would kill the intruder himself, slowly and artfully. A display for the Emperor, which would earn him recognition and riches. His heavy saber whistled through the air in a series of impressive cuts.

Semoon watched the display and knew the pirate was doomed. She had seen Tarok kill many men. Her eyes flicked to the intruder, who was still smiling! Maybe he was mad. She felt a slide of disappointment at the notion. Just as her disappointment took hold, she noticed his level stare, the slight flexing at the knees and the coiled readiness of his muscles. He seemed filled with a magnificent and primitive savagery. Ah! she thought, we have a cornered panther here. Tarok rushed in. She smiled to herself: and here comes a pampered mastiff to kill it.

Tarok's first overhead slash was a feint, intended to set his opponent up for the lightning backhand cut that would disable his sword arm. Everything was going to plan, until his opponent ignored the feint and met the supposedly unexpected cut with his own blade. The first ringing of steel-upon-steel drew an admiring gasp from the eager spectators. They, too, had seen Tarok kill many men. The giant bodyguard took a step back as his opponent's blade flicked at him like a serpent's tongue. A cut opened up on his arm. He stumbled and cursed. Then, with an inarticulate roar, he charged, putting all his strength into a series of savage, hacking blows, which the intruder met squarely. The ringing and clashing of steel transformed the tranquil ambience of the terrace to that of a busy blacksmith's shop.

In a flash, the pirate stepped inside one of the giant's mighty swings. His saber blade springing bright and clean from Tarok's back. For a moment, it remained there, vibrating slightly, before being withdrawn swiftly. Tarok crumpled like a felled ox. A seabird's cry mocked them all. Silken hangings rippled in the ocean breeze. Suddenly, with vengeful cries, the guardsmen leapt forward.

"Stop!" The pack of guardsmen slithered to a confused halt as the Princess stepped between them and their prey. She stood with her back to the intruder facing the entire gathering. "It seems as though I am in need of a new bodyguard, and who better to fulfill that role than the man who slew the old one?" she announced.

The crowd parted as the Emperor moved forward. There was a look of concern on his broad, open face. "Sister, this man is a pirate, and a northern barbarian by the look of him. He is not to be trusted. I will assign somebody more suitable."

She pouted at her brother. "Who could be more suitable than a man who can fight a battle, swim ten leagues and slay an Emperor's champion, all in the same day?"

"He is not to be trusted," the Emperor persisted.

Turning on her heel, she stepped up to the barbarian. The assembly gasped, guardsmen hefted their weapons and her brother frowned. The air crackled with tension.

She looked up at the tall northerner, her large, brown eyes searching his scarred and battered face. "Can I trust you with my life?" she asked.

Looking down at her, the corsair detected something in her face. Her arrogance had been replaced by something else. What was it? A plea, perhaps? He answered her gruffly. "More than you can with any of these painted dogs."

Sensing truth in his words, she gave him a discreet smile and swayed against him briefly. Except for her soft breasts and rounded hips, the Princess's body was slim, lean and firm. Lithe muscle flexed beneath her perfect skin. She was clad only in jeweled breastplates and a golden loin belt. Her perfume filled his nostrils. His desire flared. She spun about. Her long, rich, black hair brushed against his bare skin as she did so. He groaned softly.

"You see." The Princess held her arms wide in the shadow of the barbarian, as if she had just tamed a wild beast, which was exactly what she had done.

✝

There were twenty, powerfully built, bearers straining beneath the wide-curtained palanquin of heavily carved wood. At regular intervals, others who milled about waiting their turn, replaced them. This strategy ensured none of the burly men ever grew tired enough to stumble. In this manner, Princess Semoon floated across the hot land in a private, silken boudoir, screened from the fierce heat and impertinent stares. The big Northman accompanied the Princess's ornate litter, riding a high-stepping stallion that attempted to bite him at every opportunity. The horse had belonged to Tarok, and obviously resented the change of ownership. They were following a well-paved road that had lifted gently away from the coast and now meandered through an area of low, scrub-covered hills. The outlander eyed the surrounding sun-soaked undulations with suspicion; if he were a brigand, this would be his terrain of choice. True, they were being escorted on this journey to the city of Bansaray by a hand-picked squadron of the Emperor's lancers, but they did not impress him with their bright pennants and polished breastplates. He himself wore a dull helmet with cheek and neck guards, a mail shirt that left his arms bare and coarse leggings with high leather riding boots. On his saddle horn hung a battered metal shield with a wicked center-spike. In a scabbard under his right leg, were several throwing spears. Slung across his back was a heavy cavalry saber, which had seen good service and had thus been thoroughly tested.

"You!" called a sweet voice from beside him. "The Princess wishes to know your name."

For a moment, before answering, he regarded the speaker's pretty face, framed as it was by the palanquin's silk curtains. "Tell your mistress that I shall whisper it in her ear when she and I are alone together."

Joyfully scandalized, the face withdrew, only to appear a moment later, eyes dancing with mischief. "My mistress orders me to tell you that only in your dreams will you ever be alone with her. Now, you must tell me your name!"

He grinned back at her insolently.

"Kuda!" A rider approached, calling his name.

The handmaidens face disappeared with his name on her lips. Kuda shook his head ruefully as the young lancer reined in. "The Captain wishes to speak with you."

The Captain barely glanced at Kuda when he arrived at the head of the column. "One of my outriders has failed to report back. It may be nothing, but you'd best look to your charge."

Kuda twisted in his saddle. To the left of the column, the ground dropped away in a slope of loose rock and scree, to their right and ahead of them, rocky outcrops crowded the road. It was the perfect setting for an ambush. Dust devils danced as a sudden hot wind panted in their faces. Kuda spat. "They're just up ahead. Horses and men, lots of them."

The Captain looked at him. "How do you …?"

Kuda wheeled the stallion abruptly. "I can smell them."

Spurring the stallion back down the line of jingling horsemen, he bellowed at the bearers' overseer. "Get that litter started back down the road. Now!"

The startled overseer began shouting and laying about him with a stout cane until the palanquin stopped and the bearers began to turn beneath their burden. From somewhere, a horn brayed. Kuda hauled back on the reins bringing the stallion to a slithering halt. Jerking the beast's head around, he faced back up the road, his eyes narrowing as he watched the lancers deploying. Then the attack was upon them. Rivers of wild horsemen boiled from the surrounding rocks, each of them screaming incoherently and waving a bright blade. Kuda tugged a throwing spear free. The high-spirited stallion tossed its head and snorted, his huge, iron shod hooves pawing at the rocky ground.

The lancers met the attackers' charge in good order and, for the most part, checked it, but there were gaps. It was through one of these that a pack of raiders surged. A pounding, clattering, bellowing river of muscle and mail charging straight toward the litter.

"Now, you black-hearted bastard!" Kuda dug his heels in. The stallion, seasoned warhorse that he was, shot forward like a bolt from a crossbow. Raising himself up in the saddle, Kuda flung the spear. The hurled weapon punched into the chest of the marauder's leading steed, killing it instantly. The beast rolled forward, flinging its rider

11

and causing the following raiders to stumble and pile up behind it. Horses staggered and fell, their frail legs snapping like kindling, crashing into their fellow beasts as they tumbled. Their riders crushed between ground and saddle.

Kuda freed his cavalry saber from its scabbard just as the stallion smashed headlong into the confusion of riders. Men and beasts went down beneath the warhorse's iron hooves as, bellowing a northern war cry Kuda scythed right and left with his blade. The raiders wheeled away in terror unable to withstand the attack. This was no disciplined lancer they were facing, this was a giant berserker unleashed from some dark legend.

Covered in gore to his elbows, Kuda tried to rein in the great stallion as it kicked and bit at the air in its rage. Ahead, he could see the line of lancers beginning to buckle under the raiders' onslaught. A high-pitched scream stung his ears. Kuda tugged the stallion's head around to see bearers streaming away from the litter, which was beginning to pitch sideways.

"Hold them! Hold them!" Kuda roared angrily as he spurred toward the overseer. The man immediately joined his laborers in their headlong rush back down the road. Unable to support their burden the remaining bearers collapsed, shrieking as they were crushed beneath the heavy wooden litter as it crashed down onto the roadside.

Kuda leapt from the stallion and dashed toward the vehicle. It was now a race to see who would reach it first: him or the pack of raiders who were bearing down upon it at break-neck speed. As he drew closer, Kuda saw the litter begin moving, and, to his horror, realized that it had begun sliding down the scree slope. Screams emanated from within as the vehicle gathered speed. Kuda leapt, just managing to grab the edge of the skidding litter.

The raiders were upon them now. Horses slithered down the slope, their riders leaning far back in their saddles. A throwing axe thumped into the woodwork by Kuda's head, but he held on doggedly, despite being dragged over the loose stones at an ever-increasing rate. His helmet flew from his head, the swirling dust blinded and choked him and his ears rang with wild cries. It was only his mail shirt and leather boots that saved him from being flayed alive by the razor-sharp gravel. With a muscle-cracking effort he pulled himself up onto the madly bouncing palanquin and lurched through the flapping curtains.

Every object inside the vehicle was being thrown violently from side to side, including the Princess and her handmaiden. With a loud crash, the litter began to spin, hurling Kuda into a jumble of silk cushions. Before he could recover, a wild figure, swinging a bloody broadsword, burst through the curtains. Seeing the Princess, the swordsman roared and staggered toward her. Kuda stuck out a foot and the man went flying, just as another figure swung through the curtains. Kuda rolled to his feet, his cavalry saber hissing as it left its sheath.

All around the bouncing palanquin, horses screamed as they tumbled down the steep slope. The second figure swung a war hammer at Kuda who ducked and thrust out with his saber. The litter lurched violently, sending both men sprawling. Kuda regained his feet first, only to narrowly avoid a wild slash from the swordsman. Seizing the man's wrist, he pulled him off balance. Falling to the bouncing floor. Kuda found himself pinned beneath the heavy swordsman, his head sticking clear out of the side of the palanquin. Dropping his sword, the man began throttling Kuda with both hands. Twisting from side to side Kuda's eyes widened at the sight of a huge granite outcrop hurtling toward his head at tremendous speed. Flinging his saber aside, Kuda grabbed the swordsman's wrists firmly as he jammed his knees into the man's midriff. A quick glance to the right filled his vision with jagged rock. Heaving with his legs Kuda launched the swordsman over his head. Releasing his grip he swiftly rolled back into the racing litter. There was a heavy thud just as the shadow of the granite outcrop flickered across the curtains. Seeing the spiked war hammer descending toward his head, Kuda kept on rolling. The spikes missed his skull by inches to embed themselves in the wooden floor. Kuda rolled to his feet and smashed a mallet-like fist into the hammer wielder's face just as a horse burst through the curtains, its rider roaring defiance and swinging a great club. The animal's hooves found no purchase on the palanquin's smooth planking and, screaming fearfully, it slid along the full length of the vehicle. Kuda and the hammer wielder jumped apart as horse and rider skidded between them on its haunches. As they passed, Kuda reached out and snatched a throwing spear from the rider's scabbard. The hammer wielder freed his weapon from the floorboards just in time to be catapulted from the litter by the impact of the spear striking him in the chest. Horse and rider vanished from the palanquin in a bone splintering tangle. Shaking his head in disbelief Kuda staggered past the sprawled, screaming women to reach the front of the plunging vehicle, where he thrust his head through the torn curtains. An oath burst forth from his lips when he saw the edge of a cliff rushing toward them.

"Hold on tight!" he shouted, needlessly.

The litter soared off the cliff's edge. Its three passengers became weightless. Their screams reached a new pitch, until a bone-jarring impact and a mighty splash cut them off. Freezing water surged over the occupants of the battered palanquin as it began to spin. Spluttering and cursing, Kuda raised himself up, experiencing as he did so a desperate longing for the life of a corsair.

TWO

Kuda waded out of the water. He stood, glaring at the surrounding mountains, before turning and looking back toward the river. Behind him, both women were struggling up the bank. Behind them, the remains of the shattered palanquin lay upon the rocks. Sitting down, Kuda removed his cavalry boots and emptied them.

The Princess approached him. She seemed composed, though bedraggled. Behind her, the sobbing handmaiden collapsed to the ground. Ignoring the distraught girl, the Princess began wringing water from her long hair.

"Well, what do we do now?" she asked matter-of-factly.

"We move," Kuda answered, replacing his boots.

"Nonsense," she retorted, swinging her hair indignantly back over her shoulder. "We will wait here until my lancers arrive."

Wild cries echoed from the bluffs above them.

"Your lancers may not be the first to arrive," Kuda muttered. In one smooth movement, he rose to his feet, throwing the Princess over his broad shoulder as he did so.

Her fists beat at his back. "Put me down! I will not be handled like this."

She squirmed and twisted but Kuda held her firmly. "You cannot run over this ground in those dainty slippers Princess and we must move swiftly."

Stooping down, he scooped up the dazed handmaiden with his free arm. With a woman draped over each shoulder, he began trotting along the riverbank.

The Princess began pulling on his hair. "You oaf! You cannot possibly outrun those wild hill men whilst carrying us. You are a stranger to this country. You are no hill man."

Kuda laughed long and loud as he sped along, out-distancing their pursuers.

✝

The chamber overflowed with a darkness that seemed to bleed from the robes of its sole occupant. There was movement in that darkness but the man ignored it, his eyes turned elsewhere. The Princess had eluded him, this he knew. He also knew that fate had sent her a protector. This barely concerned him for he was sure of his powers. He even allowed himself a smile and though there was no one there to judge it, it was a ghastly thing.

✝

The fire, though well screened from the land, would glow like a beacon to those out at sea. Semoon held her hands out to the warmth while her handmaiden plaited her hair. She had given the girl this task to calm her, and it seemed to have worked. Her sobbing had ceased and her hands were steady. They were both naked, their clothes drying before the fire. She did not know where Kuda was. After setting up camp at the water's edge, he had disappeared. She was not worried though, and this amazed her. In fact, she felt much safer now than she had for a long time. For some months now her soul had been filled with a nameless dread, as though something evil was stalking her, no matter which way she turned. Even when asleep, it seemed that she could feel some dark presence standing over her bed, watching, waiting. So much so that she awoke every morning with a cry upon her lips. A slight movement at the edge of the camp caused her to look up. The firelight's flicker reflected in the eyes of the man who had stepped out of the darkness on the opposite side of the fire. Green eyes, she mused. My green-eyed barbarian. She had not heard Kuda return and her handmaiden worked on unaware of his presence.

Semoon arched her back so that her breasts thrust arrogantly at the night sky.

✝

The Emperor dismissed the wounded lancer captain and watched him limp from the audience chamber, supported by two of his men. Turning his face to the lofty ceiling, he squeezed his eyes shut.

"Does she still live?" he whispered the question.

"I believe she does, and I shall do everything in my power to discover her whereabouts," answered the old man with a wispy white beard, who stood at the Emperor's side.

"I shall pray to the Gods," the Emperor stated solemnly.

"That would be wise," agreed the old man.

With that, the young Emperor and his chief minister turned and slowly made their way across the marbled floor, the old man leaning heavily on a staff of polished wood. Liveried guards clattered to attention at their approach. The pair stopped before a wide-arched window and the young man stared, unseeing, at the mighty city that lay spread out before them, his hurt plain.

"She is my only family," the Emperor breathed. Though his face portrayed calm, there was a catch in his voice. The old man did not reply. Instead, he reached out with one hand and squeezed the young man's arm.

✝

Kuda cast a critical eye over the pirate galley that wallowed in the offshore swell. Though she was badly damaged he recognized her as the 'Shrike'. Her captain was a comrade of his. He shook his head sadly. The vessel's dark red sails were in tatters, her black, tarred hull was scorched, and, here and there, where an imperial ram-ship had caught her a

17

glancing blow, her planking had sprung. Yet, she was still floating. Even as Kuda watched, a boat was being lowered over her side.

"Who are they?" Semoon murmured, snuggling up against him, her voice drowsy with sleep.

He placed one heavy arm around her shoulders. "Friends," he answered, grinning. He had recognized the massive bearded figure standing easily in the dipping bows of the approaching rowboat. "Go and make yourself decent," he slapped her rump and spun her away before striding across the shingle beach to greet the corsairs.

"Kuda!" The bellow came across the water. "I thought you were surely dead." The speaker was a bull of a man with a shaven head and a huge belly. "I saw your galley go down in a sea of flame," he cried out jumping over the boat's side and wading ashore. The two men met in a strong embrace.

"Belsar! I never thought I'd see your ugly face again," laughed Kuda.

"You almost didn't. We escaped from that battle by the skin of our teeth. The brotherhood of the coast is scattered across the seas with the Imperial Navy hounding them. We anchored in a hidden smuggler's cove that I knew of and carried out some repairs. You were lucky that one of our lookouts spotted your signal fire. I knew it would be some unlucky crewman who had been beached, but I never expected it to be you."

Semoon and her handmaiden stepped out onto the beach. Belsar saw them and gave a low whistle. His whole frame shook with rich laughter. "I don't believe it," he spluttered.

At that moment, ear-splitting cries filled the air. Kuda wheeled about, the cavalry saber rasping from its scabbard to fill his hand. Dozens of crazed brigands erupted from the landscape. With naked blades in their fists, the snarling bandits massed together to surround the small beach.

Knowing they were trapped, Kuda cursed through gritted teeth. "I thought I'd gutted all their trackers."

The women fled toward the boat as the mob charged.

"Belsar! Get the women into the boat. I'll hold these bastards for as long as I can."

As he spoke, Kuda glanced back over his shoulder. Belsar hadn't moved. He just stood there with a wide grin on his weather-beaten face.

Kuda's eyes narrowed to murderous slits. The twist in his gut felt like betrayal, but how? Why?

A blazing fireball fell from the morning sky to burst into liquid flame amongst the hill bandits. Knots of burning figures ran to and fro, their shaggy hair and coats ablaze. Kuda turned just in time to see the catapult on the *Shrike's* fighting platform hurl another fire-basket, glowing orange and trailing burning pitch, skyward.

Belsar clapped a big hand on his shoulder. "The *Shrike* still has her teeth, my friend. Come, let us leave this unfriendly place."

✝

Semoon, once again a Princess, sat at the head of the table in the master's cabin. Kuda and Belsar relaxed in their chairs with goblets of wine in their fists and the remains of a large meal strewn before them. Belsar belched volcanically.

The Princess regarded him coolly, her lovely face expressionless. "You live well for a defeated pirate."

Belsar nodded sagely. "It takes no skill to live uncomfortably Princess, any fool can do it. But to live a full life under the most adverse of circumstances takes a lot of craft, and I am a master craftsman."

"A skill you will need, for you are fleeing from a lost cause in a boat that leaks," she countered waspishly.

"Ah, Princess." Belsar slurped more wine. "Our cause is far from lost. Though the brotherhood are scattered and reduced in number somewhat, we will regroup. It is true that our leader Ben-Alzur does, at this moment, reside in a shark's belly, but another will take his place." He raised his goblet to Kuda. "Kuda has always been a popular captain."

Semoon felt a flutter of panic. "Kuda is in my employ."

Belsar rocked back in his seat, laughing uproariously. Kuda smiled but said nothing.

Eventually, wiping tears from his eyes, Belsar managed to speak. "I always thought that royalty had no sense of humor, yet you make me cry with laughter, Princess. You are right, this boat does leak, but it is not a boat, it is a ship and it takes money to repair a ship, which brings us to the question of your ransom."

Color rose to Semoon's cheeks and her eyes stabbed at Kuda. "Am I a prisoner then?"

Ignoring the Princess, Kuda leaned forward slowly and placed his goblet on the table top. "There will be no ransom," he stated flatly.

"What!" Belsar exploded. "We have the Emperor's sister sitting here man! He would pay any price to get her back."

Kuda's level gaze never wavered. "She is not a captive."

Belsar shifted his weight, his chair creaking back an inch. "She could be," he said.

"You are my friend, Belsar. It would grieve me to kill you."

"My crew are within call."

"They would not get here in time to save your life and, as you said, I have always been a popular captain."

For a long beat, nobody moved. Then Belsar smiled and spread his hands expansively.

"You are right Kuda," he said. "We are brothers you and I. We should not speak of killing or ransom or captives.

Instead, we should be discussing rescue, reward and honored guest." He raised his goblet to the Princess.

Semoon gave him a suspicious look but nevertheless raised her goblet in return. "Deliver me back to the Emperor in Bansaray and you shall be handsomely rewarded. Maybe even pardoned."

Belsar's mouth dropped open. "Do you hear that Kuda, I shall become an honest man again."

Kuda relaxed. "The Emperor is only human, not a God. I doubt he can work miracles."

Belsar's huge frame shook with laughter. "In any event, Princess, I cannot return you to the capital as there are too many Imperial triremes patrolling the approaches. We would be sunk on sight. No, what we will do is waylay the next coaster we come across, then transfer you to her. They can have the honor of delivering you to your brother. It seems that Kuda and I must trust you in the matter of the reward."

Semoon smiled. "Kuda can collect the reward himself as he shall be accompanying me. He …" Her voice trailed away as her eyes darted from one man to the other.

Kuda regarded her without speaking. Belsar found something interesting to look at in his drink. With an inarticulate yell, she surged to her feet, flung her goblet at a bulkhead and ran from the cabin.

"Fiery, isn't she?" observed Belsar.

†

Semoon stood at the ship's rail. The cool night breeze soothed her hot skin, but her temper remained intact. Before her, a full moon laid a silvered road across the calm sea. When Kuda's muscular arms encircled her from behind she did not acknowledge him.

"Sail away with me girl," he whispered in her ear.

She melted into his embrace, tears springing to her eyes. "Girl? If only that were all I were. But I am not. I am a Princess, and I must return to my brother's side."

He squeezed her tighter. "We have a strong keel beneath us, and the ocean's stretch forever. Let them think you died in that ambush."

"I cannot. You don't understand, there is an evil stalking my brother's realm." She shivered. "I will not abandon him to it."

"Evil?" Kuda grunted, feeling his scalp crawl.

Spinning in his arms, she tilted her beautiful face up to him. "Return with me," she pleaded in a tremulous rush. "I ask you not as a Princess but as the girl you want me to be, a frightened girl who needs your protection."

"I will return with you," he answered without hesitation. Dipping his head, he kissed her long and hard before carrying her below.

THREE

Two days later, the crew of a ramshackle coaster got the surprise of their lives when corsairs waylaid them and the Princess stepped aboard, escorted by her handmaiden and a huge brooding barbarian. With a final wave from Belsar, the two vessels parted. Three days of plodding progress later, the great city of Bansaray, capital of the empire of Jijea, hove into view. Set in a bay of wooded, rolling hills, buildings of whitewashed stone and brick reflected the sunlight. Well paved streets lead away from the broad harbor and wound their way up the slopes of the tiered city toward a majestic building of shining white stone that reared against the sky. An unnecessarily fanciful construction of sweeping flutes and curves, graceful spires and flying buttresses that gleamed in the morning sun.

Standing at the rail, Semoon raised her chin toward the magnificent marble confection. "The royal palace. My home," she said simply.

Beside her, Kuda only grunted.

She glanced sideways at him. "You are not impressed?"

"I'd be more impressed by thick walls and battlements," he muttered, eyeing the numerous slender towers that lanced skyward from the marble pile for no practical reason. "How do you defend such a place?"

"We've never had to," she answered curtly.

The captain bellowed orders. Sailors scampered over tarred lines as they furled the sails and took up their positions on padded benches. Long oars, extending from both sides of the hull, rose and dipped in a practiced rhythm. The wide-bellied coaster ceased its constant wallowing as it slid past the mole and into the calmer waters of the harbor. The sailors who had reefed the sail, lingered on the yard, their eyes drinking in every detail of this safe homecoming. They passed through the crowded harbor approaching the wharfs with a slow sweep of the oars, angling for an empty slip.

As soon as they had tied up, the shocked captain of the harbor guards was made aware of the Princesses presence and a palanquin was quickly arranged. There was a speculative hum of comment from the crowds as the litter was borne through the streets toward the palace, but Kuda's purposeful stride and aura of barely suppressed savagery prevented anyone from prying too closely. On reaching the palace, the Princess leapt from the palanquin and sprang up the broad steps, closely followed by Kuda.

In a long, richly-decorated corridor, an old man in a red brocaded coat approached them. His delight was evident. "Princess! The Gods have answered my prayers."

"The Gods have indeed been kind," Semoon answered, returning his smile. She turned to Kuda. "This is Yarrabay, the Emperor's most trusted advisor."

Kuda eyed the old man but made no reply.

"Ah yes, this must be the … er, bodyguard you recruited at the sea-palace," Yarrabay responded, running his eye over the huge barbarian. "He has served you well it seems."

"Very well," Semoon gushed, bouncing with impatience. "Yarrabay, where is my brother?"

"Here!" The Emperor entered from a side corridor, amidst a flurry of nobles. Stepping from amongst them, he took his sister in a warm embrace. When he spoke, his voice was thick with emotion. "I thought I had lost you forever."

"You almost did," she answered through tears of joy. "If not for Kuda …"

"Yes. Yes, the pirate." He approached Kuda. Although the Emperor himself seemed unconcerned, the action prompted an anxious response from his guardsmen, who pressed closer, fingering their hilts.

"I owe you more than even an Emperor can repay," he admitted.

"Do not concern yourself brother. I shall reward him amply," Semoon called out mischievously. Both men grinned.

The Emperor re-joined his sister and the retinue moved off. Yarrabay fell in beside Kuda. "You are a Northman?" he enquired.

"Yes," Kuda responded curtly.

"A dour region."

"It is that," agreed Kuda.

"So much so, it surprises me that so few of your kind ever leave it."

"Civilization does not suit us."

"In what way?"

"Civilization promises everything, but gives nothing."

"Whereas in your own northern lands …?" Yarrabay prompted.

"Nobody is ever denied food or shelter."

"Such a hospitable people," the old man said archly. "Yet, they have such a ferocious reputation."

"Those who come seeking war, find it," Kuda said with finality, and ended the conversation by striding ahead of the old man.

The aging councilman followed on at his own pace. He had noted that Kuda lacked the usual thick, guttural accent of the northern clans, which was odd. Life was hard in the North, yet few of them took to wandering. Kuda was an exception. A freebooter and a soldier-of-fortune. Stroking his beard thoughtfully, he regarded the man's wide mailed back. What are you running from, barbarian?

✝

The shadows writhed. Hissing sibilance's never made for human tongue, whispered throughout the chamber. The man at its center remained very still, his unblinking gaze fixed on the creature before him. He had summoned this beast and it had come to him, ascending from the depths of an unimaginable abyss. Sweat beaded his brow, for he knew well that any miscalculation on his part would plunge him into an eternity of shrieking horror. The obscenity squatted, unmoving, its jointed legs curled beneath it. Time had no meaning. Long feelers quested uncertainly from somewhere to caress the man's face and it was only when the cold tendrils entered his nostrils and slid into his skull that the sorcerer screamed.

✝

The feast was well under way by the time Kuda decided that he liked Semoon's brother, even if he was an Emperor. The man certainly knew how to organize a debauch, he admitted to himself, glancing around the vast hall that was lit, as if it was day, by hundreds of chandeliers burning perfumed candles. For many months, he had been subsisting on the coarse fare the corsairs had provided for him. Now, his eyes shone and saliva flooded his mouth as he contemplated the culinary extravaganza spread before his eyes. There were little sucking pigs in crisp suits of golden crackling; barons of beef running with their own juices, surrounded by piles of roast potatoes; heaps of tender young pullets and pigeons, ducks and fat geese; fish from the sea, cooked a dozen different ways; tall pyramids of huge, crimson lobsters; a vast array of fruits and succulent vegetables from the palace gardens; and sherbets, custards, cakes and every sweet delight the chefs in the kitchens could conceive. The banquet was a raucous affair. Before the groaning board at which he sat, dancing girls writhed, their oiled limbs glistening in the glow of the myriad candles. Serving girls hurried along the banquet tables, setting out trays or pouring more wine. Crowds of drunken nobles staggered between wine spraying fountains, laughing and shouting at each other over the din of strident music. High overhead, largely ignored by the boisterous throng, trapeze artists performed dizzying feats, while along the center of the hall, dwarves jousted, tilting at each other from the backs of shaggy dogs, with revelers betting furiously on the outcome of each encounter.

Already replete, Kuda tore another mouthful of beef from the joint he held, and washed it down with yet another swallow of ale.

Seated next to him Semoon laughed. "You prefer coarse ale to our finest wines?"

"I prefer a lot of things to wine Princess," he answered, making a grab for her.

With sinuous ease, she swayed out of his grasp. "Later, my barbarian, later," she giggled.

"Hell's teeth, woman. How long do we have to sit here amongst all these fops?" he snarled playfully.

Yarrabay, seated on Kuda's other side, leaned over. "You do not care for our company, Kuda?" he asked, his eyes twinkling merrily in their webs of wrinkles.

Kuda was about to reply when a disturbance at the other end of the hall attracted his attention. Courtiers were streaming away from the entrance, as though frightened by something. The dancers came to an abrupt halt, sweat gleaming on their bodies. The music and noise dwindled away, replaced by an awed silence as the throng parted for a single man, who advanced through them toward the Emperor.

He was tall and powerfully built, with the wide shoulders and tapered waist of a natural athlete. His complexion was sallow, enhanced by his black hair, which hung in swinging braids to his shoulders. A close-linked suit of black mail encased him from head to foot. The metal flowed with him, with no seam or joint that Kuda could discern.

He came to stand before the Emperor. Kuda noted the crossed swords strapped to the man's back, their hilts jutting over his shoulders. The Princess's hand sought his under the table.

The Emperor stood to face the man. Though there was a look of uncertainty on the Emperor's face, his voice did not betray it. "What do you have for me, Skarasen?"

In one swift movement, Skarasen thrust his hand into the sack he was carrying and pulled out a severed head, which he swung aloft for all to see. The bearded face attached to the ragged stump of a neck stared glassily back at the stunned crowd. A dancing girl screamed and fainted, but no one moved to help her.

The Emperor merely nodded, apparently satisfied, though not a little discomfited.

Kuda nudged Semoon. "Who is he?"

Mesmerized by what was taking place, the Princess did not answer. Instead, Yarrabay responded in a low voice. "Skarasen is an assassin, one of the killer elite. Wealthy people approach him with contracts for murder, which he and his confederates carry out with great skill and discretion."

"They kill for money?" Kuda snorted in disgust.

"Come, come Kuda. You yourself are a pirate. Surely you have killed for profit?" the old patrician pointed out.

For the first time, Kuda, his eyes chips of green ice, turned toward the old man. "I have never killed anybody who did not have a blade in their hand and were prepared to use it. It seems to me that these 'killer elites' are cowards. Cowards who stab helpless people in their beds."

"The head that Skarasen is holding," countered Yarrabay, equably, "belongs to the chief of the brigands that attacked the Princess's caravan and, as you know yourself, he and his men were not helpless or lacking in blades."

Kuda turned back to find Skarasen staring directly at him. The man's eyes were strangely light colored, almost yellow, like those of a cat. The amber-colored eyes held a look of sneering contempt. Kuda felt his hackles rise. Though they locked and held eye contact for only the briefest of moments. It was long enough to establish their loathing for one another. The assassin dropped his bloody trophy to the floor and, turning on his heel, strode from the hall without uttering a word.

✝

Having dismissed his three favorite concubines, the Emperor lay replete upon his bed, snoring contentedly. Outside the chamber's door, a guard drowsed on his spear while a cockroach-like creature, the size of a domestic cat, ascended the palace's outer wall. Horny, jointed legs carried the creature's squat body swiftly toward the open window of the Emperor's bedchamber. Long, questing feelers stretched into the opulent room, inspecting and caressing every object. The squat body followed, crouching uncertainly upon the windowsill, its angular legs bunched and quivering as though on the verge of explosive action. Although, when it did move, it did so slowly, picking its course into the room with care. Once again, the trembling feelers stretched out. This time they curled over the edge of the bed to brush the Emperor's skin. Satisfied, the creature sprang to land lightly upon the silken covers, next to the sleeping man. Patiently it waited, long feelers playing lightly over the recumbent body.

✝

Semoon was also asleep, within the circle of Kuda's arms. He, however, lay awake, idly watching the rise and fall of her magnificent breasts, admiring their perfection. From the corner of his eye, he noticed a wall hanging shift in the breeze. He wondered how there could be a breeze in the room when he himself had secured every door and window. His body tensed, senses screaming danger! He hurled himself from the bed just as two crossbow bolts thudded into the space he had vacated. An unseen hand extinguished the room's single lantern. In the darkness, Kuda reached for his saber, but his fingers closed on thin air; it was gone. Biting back a flood of curses, he glided silently through the blackness. A muffled gasp told him that someone had placed a hand over Semoon's mouth. Bellowing his rage, he rushed toward the sound but someone slid a chair into his path and he went sprawling. Instantly regaining his feet, he swung up the piece of heavy furniture and flung it across the room. His aim was true and the chair smashed through a shuttered window. Moonlight flooded the bedchamber to reveal a bizarre tableau. Semoon's naked body shone white as she struggled with two men who were carrying her across the room. Another man was hurriedly reloading a crossbow while a fourth and fifth were advancing on Kuda with raised swords.

Kuda's fury rose like a tidal wave. He charged at the advancing swordsmen, dropping at the last moment to roll into their legs. They were bowled over and before they could rise, he had their throats gripped in his hands. The crossbowman swung his weapon up, took careful aim at the giant barbarian who was throttling his comrades, and pulled the trigger. Kuda swung one of his assailants around so that the bolt thumped into the man's back. Dropping the wounded man, he took the other in both hands and flung him across the room and out of the broken window. Stooping to snatch up a fallen sword, he ran at the crossbowman, who'd abandoned that weapon and drew a saber. Kuda beat down the raised saber and delivered a blow that split the man's skull down to his teeth. Tugging his weapon free he glared about the room. There was no sign of Semoon and her two assailants. Running across to the tapestry he had seen moving, he tore it from its hangers. The blank wall behind it mocked him.

✝

The Emperor rolled over in his sleep. This was the moment the creature had been waiting for. Extending its thorny legs it scuttled forward eagerly. The needle-sharp tip of one feeler entered the Emperor's flesh at the nape of his neck, instantly injecting a fast-acting numbing agent so that when the second feeler entered alongside the first, the man slept on. Its jointed legs articulated themselves around the sleeper's chest, pulling its leathery body firmly up against his back. Holding itself there in a macabre embrace the feelers plunged on, twining themselves around the cerebral cortex and probing further into the man's brain.

✝

Twenty men-at-arms hefted the huge iron candelabra, holding it like a battering ram. Kuda, now fully dressed and armed, urged them on as they struck the wall again and again. Plaster flew and brickwork sagged until he motioned for them to stop. Stepping up to the wall he kicked at it until a whole section collapsed, revealing a winding stairway. Without hesitation, he launched himself down the worn steps, descending at a run. The stairwell was lit at intervals by smoking torches set in wall sconces that must have been placed there by the kidnappers. He could hear the guardsmen clattering down the steps behind him, but did not wait for them to catch up. The walls grew slimy beneath his outstretched hands, signifying he had descended far beneath the earth. Suddenly, he burst out into an open space.

He glanced around, sword held ready. Nothing. Nothing but pressing blackness and echoing silence until the men-at-arms boiled out from the stairwell behind him bearing flaming torches. Snatching a burning torch from one, he hissed at them to be silent. After a moment, the soft lapping of water was discernible. Holding the torch aloft, Kuda moved toward the sound. Beneath his feet a rocky floor sloped gently downwards until it reached the shores of a subterranean lake. The extent of the lake remained hidden from them by the inky blackness that the torches did nothing to dispel. Kuda barked commands to search the shoreline. The men spread out until one of them let out a cry that brought everyone running. The man held a length of rope. One end was tied to a wooden post. Kuda examined the other end; it had been neatly cut with a sharp blade.

"They had a boat waiting," the guardsman intoned solemnly.

The others lowered their weapons and stared out into the unrelieved blackness. For them the pursuit was over, the Princess lost. Without a word Kuda turned his back on them, kicked off his boots, hitched up his harness of sheathed weapons and dove into the black waters.

✝

"Seal it." The Emperor's voice echoed down the concealed stairway. Roused from his bed, he had hurried directly to the scene of the abduction.

The men gathered around him exchanged startled glances. "But the Princess …" one of them began, only to quickly close his mouth when the Emperor turned a cold gaze upon him.

"Brick it up," he snarled.

†

Kuda swam in a void. The cold waters had numbed his body within moments. He felt nothing; he could see nothing. The only sounds he could hear were the ones he made himself. His fury, however, had not abated. It drove him on. A hot core within him raged at the people who had come under the cover of night to steal his woman. The fact that she was a Princess who lived in a world where nefarious dealings and assassinations were accepted as an everyday hazard, mattered little to him. She was his chosen mate, and she had been forcibly taken from him. No matter how far or how long it took, he would hunt down the kidnappers, get her back and in doing so extract a terrible retribution. It was that simple.

†

The sorcerer rested, slumped in a chair carved from black volcanic glass. Behind hooded eyes, hidden thoughts stirred. The threads were all coming together now, converging to validate his very existence on this earthly plane. Soon it would be time to summon the one. He closed his eyes reluctantly, knowing that sleep would uncage the nightmares.

†

"Light the lantern," the man working the long oar at the stern instructed.

Immediately, his companion rose, moving slowly and deliberately to the bow of the boat where he fumblingly lit the lantern that was set there. The clay oil lamp gave out a weak amber light that washed over the wooden vessel, accentuating the outer darkness that pressed in on them. Turning away from the lamp, the man's eyes fell on their bound and gagged captive, who lay naked in the bottom of the small boat. Reaching out, he stroked Semoon's thigh. She jerked and writhed at his touch.

"Keep a lookout, you fool. We should be close," the oarsman hissed in an urgent whisper.

The man looked up. "We have time."

"Yes, you are right," the oarsman answered seriously. "And when she tells Shikrol what you have done, I will spare the time to watch you being flayed alive."

The man withdrew his hand as though stung.

"There!" the oarsman pointed.

They were approaching a wall of black rock. Set in the wall, at water level, was the mouth of a tunnel. Deftly the oarsman steered for it.

Kuda saw the flare of the lantern, a mere pinpoint of light far ahead. But it was enough. He struck out in its direction with renewed vigor. A few minutes later, the light disappeared, but he had marked its position and swam on unerringly. He felt, rather than saw, the loom of the black cliff as it rose before him. As the sounds he made amplified in his ears, he knew he had entered a tunnel. Soon he was rewarded by another glimpse of the lantern light, closer now.

The oarsman fetched the wooden boat up against the steps of a stone quay. His companion jumped across with a rope and tied the boat before ascending the algae-slick stairs. Crossing a flat-paved wharf, he made his way to a stack of barrels and tipped part of the contents from one onto an unlit torch. Taking out a flint striker, he lit the fresh oil and raised the burning torch over the steps. Grotesque shadows flapped around them as the burly oarsman, who could now see clearly, hefted the Princess over his shoulder and stepped out of the boat.

Reaching the top of the steps, he spoke sharply. "Release the guardian."

"What for? There's no chance of anybody following us," the torch bearer argued.

"Do it," the oarsman spat out impatiently.

Grumbling, the man moved to an iron lever, and setting himself, heaved down on it. There was a heavy clunk of shifting counterweights and a whir of greased chains. As they watched, a huge barred gate set into the living rock of the tunnel wall, swung open. Without a word they turned hurriedly away and ran to another flight of steps which they climbed quickly, casting fearful glances back over their shoulders.

Kuda swam toward the deserted quay that was revealed to him in the moored boats lantern light. His view was interrupted when the tunnel's still waters heaved up in a swell of displaced water that lifted him to the roof. Something huge had entered the tunnel ahead of him. Filling his lungs, he dove deep into the black waters, kicking out until his chest scraped the tunnel's floor. The water pulsed against him and he had to cling to the slimy rocks to prevent himself being swept back down the tunnel. Two luminous green orbs approached out of the gloom, followed by a long, massive body that glided swiftly over him. Lungs aching, he kicked for the surface, bursting through to draw in great gulps of fetid air. A tremendous commotion shook the passage behind him. He twisted around to see a great scaled body writhing and turning, filling the tunnel and thrashing the black waters white.

With the hairs on the back of his neck rising, he struck out for the quay. Snatching a look over his shoulder he glimpsed maddened reptilian eyes swiftly bearing down upon him and vast jaws gaping wide to form a pink, tooth-lined cave. His gut clenched hard when he realized that he would not reach the safety of the wharf before the monster was upon him. Then for the second time, he felt himself being buoyed up. In the confines of the tunnel the massive creature was driving a bow wave ahead of itself. The wave smashed against the quay, flinging the Northman onto the flagged stones before receding. Kuda was left gasping.

Staggering to his feet he drew the saber that hung from his harness and glared about him. The wooden boat, still tied to the quay, was pitching wildly from side to side on the seething waters. The light from its lantern scattered crazed shadows across the tunnel walls. Chest heaving, Kuda warily backed away from the edge of the wharf. Nothing happened. Slowly, the boat's motion subsided. Kuda lowered his blade. The waters erupted as the creature launched itself onto the quay, its jaws snapping closed mere inches from Kuda's startled face. He reeled backward, swinging his saber, only for it to clang uselessly off an armored hide. Spotting a flight of curving stone steps, Kuda ran up them. Pausing at the top, he turned to get his first good look at the beast. A crocodile! Never before had he seen such a colossal reptile. Not even on the jungle-fringed rivers of the South, where the reptiles were noted for their huge size and ferocity. Its jaws were as long as a horse and as it swung its gnarled saurian head from side to side it eyed Kuda with wickedly gleaming eyes. Tensing its thick forelegs, the crocodile began pulling its entire length from the water. Kuda turned, only to find the head of the stairway blocked by a formidable looking door of black wood studded with iron nails. Spitting curses, he pushed at it. Unsurprisingly, there was no give, it had been barred from the other side. A great hissing and a rush of foul breath caused him to spin around. The huge reptile was ascending the stairs. His mind raced; he was trapped.

Sheathing his saber, he clenched his teeth and bounded down the steps. The croc saw him coming and reared up. As the creature's jaw widened in anticipation, Kuda leapt. Tucking and rolling in mid-air, he added a sudden impetus to his leap that carried him through the gaping jaws a split second before they slammed shut with a crash like a falling portcullis. Landing on his feet blade jumping into his hand he slashed down only to have his steel bounce off a hide scaled like the bark of an ancient oak. A crested tail the size of a log swung at him and he jumped high into the air. The tail swept under him to smash a stack of barrels to matchwood splashing their contents over the wharf. Without pause and incredible speed, the crocodile turned and lunged at him.

Dropping his useless saber, Kuda barely managed to twist away so that once again the jaws snapped closed on empty air. He sprang forward to lock both his arms around the creature's snout. The great saurian strained to open its jaws lifting Kuda into the air, wildly thrashing its head from side to side. Grimly, the Northman held on, the muscles in his brawny arms bulging and writhing in the flickering lamplight. Slamming him to the ground, the maddened reptile pushed him across the oil-slick paving and off the edge of the quay, swinging him out over the black water. He stared into the reptile's eyes and saw triumph there, for the monster knew that once they plunged into those murky depths he was doomed.Twisting his head to look down, Kuda saw the stone steps leading up from the water and the steady trickle of oil that ran down them from the burst barrels. At the foot of the stairs, the kidnapper's boat was still afloat. The crocodile tensed to leap. Kuda had to act fast. Releasing one arm, he jammed a thumb into the reptile's eye. It reared back, flinging its head high. Kuda let go and fell onto the stairs. Scrambling to his feet, he snatched the clay oil lamp from the boats bow and flung it onto the steps, where it smashed to pieces, unleashing its flame over the trickle of oil. A trail of blue fire swept up the stairs. When it reached the smashed barrels they exploded with a great whoosh. A ball of rolling flame swept along the quay. As a blast of heat seared his skin Kuda dived into the water. Kicking out powerfully he dove deep. The waters that closed over him were no longer black. Instead, they were brilliantly lit by the orange glow of the inferno that engulfed the tunnel. Lungs straining, he pushed himself up off the bottom to surface into a hellish world of boiling smoke and flame. Coughing and spluttering, he began swimming back to the quay. A huge fireball shot out of the conflagration to arc over his head. He had only seconds to discern the crocodile's shape amongst the flames before it splashed down to vanish in a cloud of steam.

Picking his way across the wharf between smoldering fires, Kuda retrieved his saber. The oaken door at the head of the curving steps had collapsed into a pile of charred timbers. Stepping over them, he wearily climbed the stairway beyond to find himself in a narrow alley that snaked through tightly packed houses. The warren of shabby buildings clearly meant he was in the run-down, older part of the city. Looking up, he could see the crimson streaks of dawn stretching across the sky. Of the Princess, there was no sign.

FOUR

Standing shoulder-to-shoulder, Jijea's aristocracy, city elders, wealthiest merchants and military leaders were packed into the royal palace's high-ceilinged audience chamber. Noblemen and courtiers jostled each other, vying for places, vying for attention in finery all the colors of the rainbow. The air was still and stuffy, the scent of clashing perfumes overwhelming. Without explanation, the Emperor had summoned them to the palace. Speculation vibrated through the throng of people like an unseen cataract. A phalanx of palace guards formed a human screen between the crowd and the dais, on which the empty throne sat. Yarrabay stood at the front of the gathering, his grey beard wagging as he fielded the many enquiries being directed at him. Though he could offer no clue as to the reason behind the Emperor's summons.

The Emperor entered through a door behind the throne, without fanfare. All heads turned toward the raised dais. He stepped up to the edge of the black marble platform and surveyed the tightly packed assembly. Steadily, the murmuring died away to be replaced by an expectant hush.

In loud ringing tones, the Emperor commenced speaking. "Princess Semoon has been found guilty of plotting my death, and has been imprisoned by my order."

There was instant uproar. Nobody in that crowded hall believed that their beloved Princess was capable of such an act of treason. Loudly, they voiced their opinions.

The Emperor, seemingly unperturbed, waited for the waves of protest to recede before continuing. "The evidence cannot be denied, and I am convinced of my sister's guilt." He raised an arm to quiet more protests. "My sister's treachery was uncovered by the new high priest of Jijea."

He turned and gestured to a tall, dark-robed and hooded figure. Until now, the figure had stood, unnoticed, by the throne. Exuding menace the cowled man strode forward to be greeted by a hostile silence. The stranger drew back his hood to reveal chilling black eyes that swept the gathering with glowering enmity.

The Emperor introduced him. "Shikrol!"

At that moment, beyond the high windows, a cloud passed before the sun. The gathering moved restlessly. The hall dimmed. The silence deepened so that though he barely moved his thin lips, Shikrol's voice carried to every corner of the vast chamber.

"The traitoress will be publicly executed at the opening of the summer games," he announced with a note of gloating triumph in his voice. That said, he made as if to turn away, but, as though struck by an afterthought, he turned back to face the gathering. "By me," he added in a voice that was malevolence incarnate.

†

Yarrabay hurried from the audience chamber, which was in an uproar, refusing to answer any of the angry questions fired at him. Reaching his chambers in another wing of the vast palace he slammed and bolted the door before slumping into a chair. His mind was working furiously. He recalled Shikrol of old. A petty schemer. One who had been banished from the court for dabbling in the black arts. Now he had returned, and by means of some dark sorcery bent the Emperor to his will. Yarrabay knew that spells of such power could only be countered by the casting of stronger spells, but the practice of magic had been outlawed in Jijea for a hundred years. There were no enchanters within five hundred miles of the city, and the midsummer games began in ten days' time. Cursing the enlightened times he lived in, the old man beat a liver-spotted fist impotently on the arm of his chair. Then he caught himself and, taking a deep breath, forced his mind to think rationally. He could always take out a contract with the killer elite for Shikrol's death, but would the spell die with him?

A sudden loud banging shook the chamber's door in its frame, causing the old man to leap to his feet. So soon, he thought, scowling at the vibrating wood. Shikrol was not wasting any time in disposing of anyone who could oppose his schemes. First the Princess, and now him. Squaring his bony shoulders, he unbolted the door. It crashed back on its hinges and Kuda stormed into the room.

"Hell's teeth!" the barbarian raged, scarcely sparing the oldster a glance before snatching up a flagon of rare wine and draining it. Wiping his mouth with the back of his hand, he went on to attack a bowl full of fruit.

"I need a thousand men-at-arms to cordon off a section of the old city," he ordered between bites. "I trailed the Princess's kidnappers there. We need to seal the place off before beginning a house to house search."

Yarrabay stared, wide-eyed, at the half-naked barbarian. Although his huge frame was filthy, scorched and lacerated, his eyes still blazed with vitality and iron purpose. A glimmer of hope began to stir in the old council-man's breast. Here was a random element that hadn't been factored into Shikrol's calculations. An anomaly with the implacable, unswerving purpose of an attack hound.

"I know where the Princess is," he spoke quickly.

Kuda's head snapped up, a puzzled frown knitting his brow.

"Where?"

"She is here, in the palace dungeon."

"What!" Kuda roared, sending a stream of pulped fruit across the room. Tugging his heavy cavalry saber free he charged toward the door.

Moving with surprising speed for one so ancient, Yarrabay managed to slam and bolt the portal before the barbarian reached it.

"Out of my way, you old fool," Kuda growled leveling his sword threateningly.

Trying to ignore the great blade, the old man held up his hands. "If you attempt to free the Princess now, you will be killed and she will die." He gulped. "You must listen to me."

Slowly, the blade lowered. Yarrabay lost no time in telling Kuda everything that had occurred that morning. At the end of the account, Kuda began pacing the room like a caged tiger, his brows knotted in thought.

"How many of the citizens are for the Princess?" he asked suddenly.

"All of them," the old man answered immediately. "Without a doubt. But their loyalties are divided as they also love the Emperor. And he commands the army and navy."

"Weaklings!" Kuda spat in disgust.

"They are confused and it would take months to organize any resistance to the Emperor's will. We only have ten days to act." Yarrabay shook his head despondently. "We need to find a powerful sorcerer to help us counter Shikrol's dark magic."

Kuda stopped mid-pace to scowl down at the old man. "Let me tell you something about sorcery, you old fool. It thrives upon discord and strife, growing until it consumes all that it touches. Were you to invite more sorcerers here, Jijea would never be free of their malevolence."

Yarrabay slumped back into his chair, a surge of despair overwhelming him. "Then we are lost," he said softly.

"Lost," Kuda snorted, eyeing the old man scornfully. "How civilization weakens a man's spirit. We have not even begun to fight and already you are defeated." His eyes turned steely. "We know the Princess is alive, and we know her whereabouts. We even know the time of her execution. Now, what of the place?"

The old chief minister sat forward in his chair. "The Heronium Stadium," he answered quickly. "Down by the river. Are you familiar with the stadium?"

Kuda nodded. "I have seen it. A vast construction."

"Ancient too," Yarrabay went on, one thin-fingered hand absently stroking his grey beard. "In the dark ages, it was a place of death matches and human sacrifice. Those stones have seen much blood."

"They're going to see a lot more, old man, a lot more," Kuda promised grimly.

†

As the silken robes slithered to the floor, Shikrol took a sharp intake of breath. The Emperor stood naked before him, revealing the incubus. The reed-thin sorcerer moved in a slow, careful circle around the Emperor, examining the beast as he did so. The creature's body had flattened itself against its host's backbone, and he could see where feelers had plunged their full length through the skin. The flattened body pulsated slightly. Chitinous legs adjusted their grip, making clicking sounds as they moved. Satisfied, Shikrol used his mind to instruct the Emperor to dress quickly. The young man did so, concealing the creature beneath his voluminous robe.

Shikrol smiled, still amused by the novelty of controlling the Emperor with his mind through the incubus. The sorcerer's merest whim was the Emperor's command, which meant that he, Shikrol, the former outcast, was now the ultimate power in Jijea. A sorcerer could never become Emperor, he knew that. Certainly not over a people who shunned the dark arts, but a skilled practitioner of black magic could hold the throne and the loyalty of its subjects, providing he pulled the strings that made a royal puppet dance. His eerie smile widened at the thought. Though, Jijea itself was only a tool to be used in summoning the one. When he sacrificed the Princess in ten days' time, her royal blood would begin a chain reaction that would engulf this entire plane of existence. Brow creased in thought, the smile faded as the sorcerer rubbed one long-fingered hand over his shaved pate. Such a reaction, however, required a great deal of energy, especially at the outset. Shikrol licked his lips with a long, dog-like tongue. The Heronium Stadium would be packed with one hundred thousand people. More than enough sustenance for the one.

✝

The shadows in the palace gardens were hung with mingled fragrances of shrub and blossom. The scent of lotus and jasmine spiced the cool night air. Two figures used those shadows to make their way through the manicured shrubbery unobserved. Upon reaching the palace's boundary wall, they paused.

"There is a hidden door here somewhere, if only I can find it," Yarrabay muttered, pushing at various bricks.

Kuda, wrapped in a dark cloak, loomed at his shoulder. "You had best come with me old man. If you stay here, your life will not be worth a tinker's curse."

"You are probably right, Northman," agreed Yarrabay, continuing with his search. "However, I cannot abandon the Emperor and the Princess. The evil forces that are preying upon them are, I suspect, even more powerful than Shikrol comprehends. My continued presence will, I hope, bring some small comfort to the Princess." A brick moved under his touch. "Ah! I have it." A section of the wall swung silently open on oiled pivots.

Moving the old man aside, Kuda craned his neck through the opening to find himself looking down a deserted, dimly-lit street. He drew back. "You have courage, old man."

"For a fop," Yarrabay replied archly.

Kuda's grin flashed white in the darkness. "If you manage to speak with the Princess, tell her that I have not forgotten my promise to the girl on the *Shrike*." Then he was gone.

Using streets and cross-alleys that were little frequented and only poorly lit, Kuda made his way to the waterfront. Here, there were crowds, for the commerce of this great port did not cease with the setting of the sun. There was much traffic at the harbor, with coast barges, skiffs, and big fishing boats coming in with their catch. Shouldering his way through the throng, Kuda stepped into a side street lined with taverns. When he came to one that was set back a little from the others, he ducked through the doorway. Pushing his way across the smoky interior, his head brushing the low ceiling, he chose a corner table and sat down. Looking morosely around the room, he took in the low ceiling of smoke-blackened beams and the uneven flags that made up the floor. He noted that the clientele were predominantly seafaring men, who were mostly drunk and raucously entertaining themselves with the local harlots. Kuda surveyed them with interest, his keen eyes missing nothing. The place sang with noise: laughter, shouts, cries for more wine and the giggling of the flirting, half-naked strumpets. The room stank of their sweat, mingled with the discernible odors of wine, ale and cooking food. Tobacco smoke hung thick in the air. On one wall, a small boy was seated, turning the handle of a spit on which, over an open fire, a pig was roasting. An overworked serving wench approached and without a word, slammed a tankard of foaming ale on the table in front of him. He flipped her a copper coin, which she deftly caught before twirling away. He had time for only one swallow before a fulsome shape slid onto the bench next to him.

"Buy me a drink, lover?" the girl asked with a sly, cheeky grin.

He leaned toward her and whispered something in her ear that caused her to giggle and wriggle in no particular order.

†

Yarrabay bowed deeply and approached the throne, his staff tapping once on the marble floor of the audience chamber for every step he took. The seated Emperor watched him approach, his face a pale wedge of indifference. A scribe sat cross-legged beside the throne, his palette and pens prepared. Yarrabay knew that every word would be recorded so that, if needed, it could be used later to condemn the speaker. Shikrol hovered close by, his chilling gaze fixed upon the old man.

Drawing nearer, Yarrabay was disconcerted to see how ill the Emperor looked. The open and youthful face everyone knew and loved, had undergone a change. The once vigorous features seemed to have dissipated; the skin stretched too tight over the bone. Dark circles ringed the eyes. Masking his concern, the old councilor drew himself up to address the throne.

"Sire, I must protest at the cruel treatment of your beloved sister."

"No longer beloved," the young man's voice rasped, as though it were being forced painfully through protesting vocal cords.

Yarrabay winced at the sound of that mangled voice. Something in its awfulness told the old man more than words ever could that the Emperor would not survive the warped magic that gripped him. With that realization came a renewed surge of hatred for Shikrol.

"That creature," he pointed his staff at the sorcerer, "has no business at this court. He was banished years ago and should never have been allowed to return."

"He returned to uncover a plot against my life," the Emperor intoned, passionlessly.

"Where is the evidence?" Yarrabay was looking directly at Shikrol now. "Why has it not been presented to the court?"

"The evidence has been presented to me," the young man grated. "And I am satisfied with its validity."

Although it was the Emperor who spoke, the elderly statesman had the uncanny feeling that Shikrol was the one responding to his questions.

"The investigation is ongoing, and it would be unwise to reveal too much at this stage," the Emperor droned on.

Shikrol thrust his head forward like a vulture smelling carrion. His gleaming eyes fixed upon the chief minister.

"There are more plotters to uncover," the Emperor finished.

✝

Growing ever more impatient, Kuda drained another flagon of ale. The girl seated next to him made a lewd suggestion, which he ignored. He knew the inn to be the haunt of a brotherhood spy, who regularly informed the corsairs as to which vessels carried the richest cargoes. While Kuda did not know the man by sight, the informant would certainly recognize Kuda. He had been waiting for two hours, but nobody had approached him. The girl squeezed his thigh. She was growing impatient too, he realized. Maybe she knew the whereabouts of the spy he sought.

He looked down into her pretty, upturned face. "I am looking for a man who has contacts within the brotherhood of the coast," he told her in a low voice. "Perhaps you know of him, the pirates call him the Weasel," Kuda finished, raising his tankard to his lips.

"Why, Captain Kuda, you are speaking to her," she smiled brightly.

Kuda spat a mouthful of ale across the room, directly into the face of a giant black man.

"You!" He stared at the girl with a dumbfounded look upon his face, until a black fist the size of a beer keg, wiped it off.

The bench went over backward and the table went up in the air. The girl fell to the floor and crawled across the stained paving, between milling legs until she reached the tavern door, which she quickly slipped through.

Once outside, she stood listening to the sounds of the tavern being torn apart. A bench smashed through a window closely followed by the unconscious black man.She heard Kuda bellowing above the uproar.

"Hah! Blades is it, you sons of whores, and I was going to keep it friendly!"

Three sailors crashed through the door wearing a heavy table. Painted doxies ran screaming into the street. A throwing knife embedded itself in the doorjamb. A chorus of meaty smacks culminated in a bloodcurdling scream. Through a window, she could discern the flicker of flames.

Then Kuda, bloody blade in hand, stood framed in the doorway. "Come on, girl," he said, taking her by the arm and dragging her along the street. "I would never have suspected that you were the Weasel."

"Perhaps we have different interpretations of the word 'undercover'," she responded, eyeing the wreckage of the tavern.

FIVE

The dungeon keeper led the way along a damp and moldering passageway. Yarrabay followed, a perfumed handkerchief pressed to his nose. Oily smoke issuing from animal fat torches curled lazily along the low, curved ceiling, adding to the stench of unwashed bodies and human waste. Stopping before an iron door, the dungeon keeper fumbled with a bunch of keys before selecting one and inserting it into the keyhole. After working the lock, he pulled the door open and stood back. Yarrabay moved past him. Taking one step over the threshold, he froze, a gasp of disbelief escaping his lips at the sight that met his eyes.

Dim light from the corridor spilled into the dark cell to illuminate the Princess, who hung naked in chains.

Biting down on his anger, Yarrabay spoke. "Posan, how is little Amelia?"

The dungeon keeper hung his head and muttered a reply. "She is well, Lord."

"Do you remember when she was ill with the flux?" the old man went on."When she almost died."

"Yes, Lord."

"Do you recall who brought the royal physician to your house?"

"You did, my Lord."

"I would ask that you bring me something now, Posan."

Posan lifted his head, his eyes bright with tears of shame. "Anything, my Lord."

"Food, clothing, clean straw for a bed and the keys to those chains."

Semoon sat on a pallet of fresh straw, her horror growing steadily as Yarrabay told her of her brother's accusation and Shikrol's pronouncement.

"Lies! All lies," she snapped angrily.

"Of course." The old man took her hands in his, patting them reassuringly. "I do not believe that your brother's actions are his own. Shikrol has ensnared him in a web of sorcery that has reduced him to little more than a marionette."

"Then we must break the enchantment," she said hurriedly.

"Indeed, we must," Yarrabay nodded in agreement. "And I am doing everything I can. But I am no sorcerer, and Shikrol's powers have grown somewhat since his banishment."

Semoon stared disbelievingly at the wise old man, who had been her protector and friend since childhood. Her voice, when she spoke, sounded small and fearful, even to her own ears. "Are you saying that all is lost?"

Squeezing her hands tightly, he looked into her frightened eyes. "There is one hope. Kuda, the barbarian, sends you a message. He would have you know that he has not forgotten the girl on the *Shrike*."

The effect of his words was miraculous. Semoon's depression evaporated before his eyes. Suddenly energized, she sat up straighter. "My green-eyed outlander!" she exclaimed. "He lives! Where is he?"

"Abroad in the city somewhere. He told me to wait, and that he would contact me soon." The old man peered at her in the dim light. Seeing the new hope on her face, he sighed heavily. "Please, Princess, do not put too much faith in a footloose barbarian. As we sit here, he could be fleeing the city on a stolen horse."

She shook her head vigorously, long, black hair swirling. "How little you know him."

†

At that moment, the Weasel was leading Kuda down a dark alleyway. The alley veered sharply and widened, becoming a small irregular square. She stopped by a closed door and hitched up her skirts to display shapely legs.

The Northman shook his head. "We don't have time for that, girl."

"Calm yourself, captain." She reached down to pluck a key from a leather pouch that was strapped to her thigh. Turning away from him, she used the key to unlock the door. Pushing it open, she passed through, motioning for him to follow.

"Close the door behind you," she instructed, her voice coming from the pitch blackness beyond the portal. Light flared as she lit a lamp.

Closing the door, Kuda found himself in a low-ceilinged room. It was clean, neat and full of feminine touches.

She made a sweeping gesture. "Welcome to my home."

"My thanks." He allowed himself a smile. "Do I call you Weasel or do you have a real name?"

"My given name is Ariane." Her thick, golden hair shone in the lamplight as she crossed to sit on the bed. "Why were you seeking me, Kuda?"

"I need you to carry a message to Captain Belsar of the *Shrike*," he answered, moving further into the room.

"That is easily done," she nodded, her eyes flirting with him.

"I shall see to it that you are rewarded," he said, looking down at her.

She leaned back on the bed to look up at him. "Personally?" A hint of amusement tugged at the corners of her mouth.Her fingers began pulling at the strings of her too-tight bodice.

"Personally," he confirmed, aware of his body's sudden reaction as he watched her release her full breasts from their confinement. Stooping forward, he put his left arm around

51

her waist and pulled her up against him, kissing her full on the mouth. There was no hesitation in her lips as she melded against him. Her mouth opened, her tongue darting against his.

When their lips parted, she was breathing sharply and there was an urgency in her eyes. "Perhaps you'd like to give me something in advance," she said huskily.

Her skirts landed at his feet a split second before his harness full of weapons crashed to the floorboards.

†

There had been no slaves in Jijea for five hundred years. Until now. Suddenly, the Emperor decreed that anyone suspected of sympathizing with those plotting against him, were to be arrested and sentenced to hard labor. And they were. Thousands of men and women now toiled in the hot sun beneath the barbed whips of brutal overseers. As the sun's heat crushed down upon them, they worked to dismantle the city's finest buildings. The massive blocks of dressed masonry thus obtained were hauled over rollers by long lines of harnessed humanity, all the way to the massive portals of The HeroniumStadium. Once through the stadium gates, engineers working under Shikrol's direction, erected them to precise instructions. Nobody knew what they were building, they only knew that it was a monstrous and unearthly construction.

From the relatively cool shadows of the stadium's royal enclosure, Shikrol gazed out over the smooth sands of the amphitheater to where the edifice was taking shape. Piles of masonry and scaffolding littered the arena. Nervous under his gaze, the laborers used ropes, pulleys and sheer numbers to maneuver the blocks of cut and dressed stone onto rollers so they could be dragged into place. Every now and then, there would be a spurt of dust and a dull thud, muffled by distance, as a granite block slid into its prepared hole. These were the foundation stones that would support the growing monolith. Shikrol winced in the bright glare. Sunlight did not agree with him. He retreated further into the shadows joining the Emperor, who sat staring at nothing. The sorcerer ran his deep-set eyes over the seated figure. Jijea's ruler had aged fifteen years in the last week alone. All traces of the young Emperor's vitality had been eaten away from within, by some consumption beyond human naming. Shikrol was well aware that the incubus was killing the young man. No, more than that, it was devouring his soul. He just hoped that it was not doing so too quickly. He had no direct control over the beast, but that did not matter. When the one arrived, nothing would matter.

✝

With halberds shouldered, the platoon of night watchmen clumped down the street. It was the end of their shift and the men's thoughts had already wandered homeward ahead of them, so that in the deepening twilight, the figure standing silently in a darkened doorway went unnoticed. After they had passed the hidden man emerged from the darkness and stole across the street to drop into the shadows at the base of the high wall that surrounded the palace gardens. Placing his hands on a specific brick, he pushed. The brick moved and, with a barely audible click, a section of the wall sprang open. The camouflaged door opened on greased pivots, just as it had done for Yarrabay. Kuda grinned and slipped through into the gardens, securing the door behind him. Keeping his back to the wall, he paused and looked around, allowing the gloom to thicken. The breeze, perfumed with orange blossom and lilac, brushed his face. He cocked his head to listen; nothing. Although, since his last visit, an eerie atmosphere seemed to have descended upon the garden. It sent an involuntary shudder through the Northman. Ahead of him, graceful and majestic, loomed the palace. Its soaring ramparts and slender towers were backlit by the countless torches left burning through the night. Setting off, he moved silently through the well-kept grounds, avoiding paths of crushed rock and a stone-rimmed pool, covered in a carpet of water-lilies.

He came to a small, bronze-girt door, which he knew led directly into the palace. Inserting the key Yarrabay had given him, he turned the lock and swung the door open, then quickly passed through. He found himself in a cool, faintly-hushed passageway with yet another door at the far end. The door was unlocked. He eased it open a crack to peer through. He was looking down the entire length of a richly decorated hallway. He stepped into the hallway, closing the door softly behind him. His ears strained to catch the slightest sound, but there was nothing. Satisfied, he set off, cat-footed, along the polished marble floor. Paintings depicting myths and legends adorned the walls, all artfully lit by scented tapers. He kept going until he reached an open archway that led into a cavernous circular room, which he assumed to be the base of one of the palace's many towers.

A large statue of some legendary heroic warrior slaying a dragon dominated the center of the room. Kuda skirted this ostentatious monument to begin climbing a flight of wide, curving stairs. He froze mid-step when he heard voices approaching. Without hesitation, he leapt onto the stairway's wide, wooden banister. Straddling the polished wood, he slid down, gathering speed and momentum, before shooting off the bottom to roll into the shelter of the statue's plinth.

Two richly attired noblemen descended the stairs, oblivious to everything but their conversation. "The library of Capsis!" exclaimed the first.

"It is being torn apart even as we speak," confirmed the second in a lower voice. "They work through the night you know," he added.

"What of the ancient scrolls and books?" spluttered the first.

"Thrown into the streets. Irreplaceable and priceless works, the wisdom of ages strewn upon the cobbles."

"This is an outrage!" shouted the first.

The second noble waved him to silence as they reached the foot of the stairs. "Have a care," he hissed. "The new high priest has long ears." He looked around fearfully. "You could be branded a rebel and forced to work in the dismantling of our great public buildings yourself."

They moved further into the room. Kuda had to shift around the statue's plinth to remain out of sight. Their conversation carried on in lower tones. "What is he constructing?"

"Nobody knows and nobody dares to enquire. But it is not a building as we know it. There are no chambers doors or corridors, just a great pile of interlocking stone blocks that rises ever higher in the center of the stadium."

"These are stressful times," muttered the other darkly.

At the sound of approaching footsteps, the two men stopped talking. Kuda cursed under his breath, the palace was as crowded as a marketplace at midday. The newcomer would see Kuda as soon as he entered the chamber as he was in plain sight of the entrance that the footsteps were coming from but if he moved, the noblemen would spot him.

Reaching an unspoken agreement, the two nobles moved quickly toward an exit, away from the approaching footsteps. Wasting no time, Kuda eased himself silently around the square plinth. The two noblemen had their backs to him as they left the chamber. As they exited, the newcomer entered from the other side. Out of sight once again, Kuda listened to the new arrival's footfall. They came to a halt on the opposite side of the plinth. Once again, the big barbarian breathed a curse, his patience was wearing thin. The footsteps resumed as the man set off across the chamber, heading for the same exit the nobles had departed from. Kuda eased around the sides of the plinth yet again, remaining out of sight. When the man had gone, he lost no time in sprinting up the stairs, three at a time.

Reaching the upper levels, he followed a tastefully tapestried and carpeted corridor until he came to the familiar door of Yarrabay's ornate chambers. The door opened to his touch. The old man should be less trusting, thought Kuda as he entered. Moving silently through the dark rooms, he found the ancient councilman in the largest chamber. The old man was facing away from him. Kuda whistled softly. The oldster's ears were sharp for he turned immediately at the sound, his face a pale oval in the gloom. The old man hesitated a moment before moving toward the big Northman, his head bobbing in a curious fashion. Observing his irregular gait, Kuda smiled to himself. The old fart is drunk, he surmised. The smile froze on his face as Yarrabay drew closer. There was no body beneath the bobbing head, just the bloody stump of a severed neck and the fingers of a black mailed fist entwined in the grey hair.

†

With an inarticulate cry Kuda surged forward, his saber jumping from its scabbard, swift as a striking adder. The blade of a short sword rose from the dim shadows to block his first cut. Faster than summer lightning Kuda swung a backhand slash, which met with no resistance as an indistinct figure swayed backward, just out of reach of his questing blade. Yarrabay's decapitated head flew at him. Kuda ducked to almost meet his doom as a second blade sliced upward toward his neck. Only his panther-like reactions saved him from the old man's fate. Having rid himself of the councilman's head the murderer slid like a wraith from shadow to shadow, weaving a lethal pattern with a pair of short swords. Kuda suddenly recognized his opponent. That realization stoked the fires of his rage. He struck again and again faster than the eye could follow. Yet, each of his attacks was turned aside with almost contemptuous ease.

Chest heaving, the Northman took a step backward, careful to keep himself between the murderer and the only exit. His adversary stepped into the light from the doorway, confirming Kuda's realization. Skarasen smiled like a content cat, adding more fuel to the furnace of Kuda's hatred. Forcing himself to remain calm, the tall barbarian took a firmer grip on the hilt of his saber and with his other hand drew a long-bladed knife from a sheath at the small of his back.

"Only one of us will leave here alive, assassin," he snarled through gritted teeth.

"I know," Skarasen replied, emotionlessly.

The attack came in a blinding flurry of razor-edged blades that somehow managed to take Kuda by surprise. The outlander gave no ground and met the attack with blades of his own, filling the apartment with a cacophony of ringing steel. The assassin's left hand blade flashed low, seeking an opening. Kuda shifted his weight and blocked. Instinct, refined in hundreds of sword fights, told him that this was a feint, so he kept moving, falling into the parry instead of recovering. Skarasen's hissing right hand blade shaved the hair from his head instead of severing his neck. Rolling to the ground, Kuda rolled a second time before springing to his feet, just in time to see the black-mailed figure disappearing through the doorway.

Spitting curses, Kuda gave chase while noting that Yarrabay's head was gone. Storming through the chambers, he stopped short at the door. The corridor stretched away, empty in both directions. There was no sign of the assassin. From one direction, however, came the sound of pounding feet and shouted orders. The palace guard had been called out. Whirling around, he sprinted in the opposite direction.

The corridor debouched onto a raised gallery that ringed a long narrow banqueting hall. Kuda spotted the assassin immediately. He was running along the gallery directly across from him, on the other side of the hall. At the center of the hall, an elaborate candelabra hung, suspended from the high ceiling on sturdy chains. Without pausing in his headlong rush out of the corridor Kuda leapt over the balustrade at full stretch and grabbed the candelabra with both hands. His impetus swung the chains just enough to carry him across the hall. Releasing his grip at the top of the swing he landed on the opposite gallery, a mere two steps behind the fleeing assassin.

Skarasen spun about violently, braided hair lashing at his contorted face, twin blades scything toward the barbarian. Kuda leapt back, cheating death by a whisker, and drew his saber. Once again, steel clashed on steel, filling the gallery with its ringing echoes. Bellowing voices announced the arrival of the palace guard, but Kuda would not allow himself to be distracted, knowing full well how Skarasen would make him pay for anything less than total concentration. A crossbow bolt zipped between the two men, but they ignored it. Behind him, a tumult of clanking metal and labored breathing told Kuda that the guardsmen were fast approaching. Caught between two enemies, Kuda had no choice but to step back from the assassin and lower his blade. Skarasen smiled his lizards smile before spinning away to swiftly disappear down another passageway, the canvas bag containing Yarrabay's head swinging from his belt.

His face a mask of fury, Kuda pistoned his left leg backward to smash the leading guardsman in the midriff. Lifted off his feet, plate armor buckled and bent, the burly guard smashed backward into his fellows. Kuda spared the tangled pile of guardsmen only a brief glance before ducking into another side corridor and racing away. The passageway ended in a large antechamber, where Kuda found himself faced by a pair of solid looking double doors, of dark, oiled wood. The doors were firmly closed and flanked by two guards. Seeing him skid to a halt before them, they lowered their halberds and charged. Side-stepping the first halberd's point Kuda made a reverse slash that opened the man's throat. He fell, gurgling, to his knees, blood jetting from his open throat. The second guardsman swung wildly. Ducking under the swinging halberd's axe blade, Kuda lunged forward and rammed a foot of honed steel down, past the edge of the man's cuirass. The hunting knife split the man's collarbone and skewered his heart. The sounds of angry pursuit echoed through the corridor behind him. His only means of escape was through the doors, so he put his shoulder to them and heaved. Formidable as they were, they swung open easily on well-oiled hinges. Kuda plunged through, slamming the oaken portals closed behind him. He glanced around, sword ready, and saw a locking bar leaning against the wall. Snatching it up, he slid it into place before catching his breath. Slowly turning, he found himself staring directly into Yarrabay's dead eyes. Bellowing a startled curse, Kuda glared about wildly. He was alone in a large room containing a long polished table on which the old man's head had been placed. Cautiously, he edged into the room. Hearing a noise, he looked up to see a group of richly attired men filing onto a high gallery that ran along one wall. They were all staring down at him with grave expressions.

One man, hollow-eyed and pale as a ghost, spoke up. "You see, good nobles. The murderer condemns himself." He gestured at the blood-spattered barbarian who was glaring up at them. "Blade in hand, and councilor Yarrabay's head horrifically displayed."

The emotionless voice dropped the words into the room. Recognizing the speaker, Kuda's throat tightened. Standing before the group of high-ranking nobles, his cadaverous frame barely able to stand upright, the Emperor swayed. While at his shoulder hovered a skull-faced shadow.

Kuda shook his notched blade in defiance. "Lies! All lies, you sons of whores." With a roar, he took three running steps to vault onto the table. As he did so, Shikrol raised a short anthracite tube to his thin lips and blew. The tiny envenomed dart flew true and the enraged Northman measured his length upon the table top.

SIX

Semoon found sleep elusive, but she must have dozed because the sound of footsteps approaching her cell door jarred her out of a light slumber. Instantly alert, she rose to her feet in a single lithe motion. The footfalls paused. She saw movement through the small barred window that was set into the thick door.

A man's voice issued from the dark aperture. "Princess."

Cautiously, she advanced toward the door. "Who's there?" she whispered.

She stopped, listened carefully and heard movement beyond the window. The black rectangle brightened, as though a lantern were being unshuttered. In the growing illumination, she could make out a face pressed up against the bars, its sagging features surrounded by a halo of shaggy grey hair. "Yarrabay!"

With a joyous cry she ran to the door, reaching it just as the light faded. She grasped the bars and peered out into the gloom. "Yarrabay! Show yourself," she commanded.

The light flared again. Yarrabay stared back at her, his dead eyes full of accusation. The severed head had been stuck onto a pole and set a few feet away from the door. No one else was in sight.

Semoon gripped the bars with both hands, her knuckles turning white. Her eyes widened as a sickening lurch of horror swept through her. Her lips quivered and then she screamed. Whirling away from the door, she threw herself full-length upon the straw that lay matted across the floor. She lay there, covering her face with her hands as great sobs of misery and grief wracked her body.

Outside the cell, mocking laughter echoed around the dank stone walls.

✝

With their hob-nailed boots pounding the cobbled street, a platoon of guardsmen in iron helms and dull cuirasses escorted a coffle of chained prisoners toward the harbor. The officer in charge strode ahead, his glower parting the crowds that thronged the avenue. After taking one look at his stern features, and noting the iron studded club he brandished, people needed little encouragement to step aside. The prisoners shuffled along sullenly behind him, fettered ankle and wrist, their bodies bowed with heavy chains.

"Rufus," a sweet voice called out the officer's name.

Jaw set in a grim line, club twitching in his hand, Rufus jerked his head around. Ariane stepped out of the crowd, a beaming smile upon her comely face. Instantly, the officer's granite features softened and the club drooped, forgotten in his hand.

"Rufus, I've been looking for you everywhere. Have you been avoiding me?" she pouted.

Rufus held up a clenched fist and the coffle came to a clanking halt behind him. "No, of course not, Ariane. I have been attending to my duties. These are busy times."

She swayed forward. His eyes obediently fell to her perfect breasts, thus presented for his inspection by an artfully low-cut bodice. He swallowed heavily.

Huge blue eyes stared up at him. "After our last night together, I thought you would have been only too eager to visit me again," she simpered, heaving a despondent sigh that caused Rufus to almost drop his club.

"Of course I want to see you again," he stammered. "But my duties …"

"Your duties," she cut him off. "Perhaps you prefer the company of these creatures to mine." She made a dismissive gesture toward the chained prisoners. "Who are they anyway? What is so important about them? Where are you taking them?"

"They're convicted criminals, thieves and murderers," he blurted out. "They are under sentence to the galleys for life. I'm taking them to the harbor."

She seemed unimpressed. Flicking a curtain of luxurious fair hair over one shoulder, she spun away. "It's entirely up to you, Rufus. However, I will not wait forever. There are other handsome guard captains in this city, you know."

He stood, face despondent, staring at her retreating posterior as she sashayed off into the crowd. A loud cough from his sergeant brought him back to his senses. Straightening his back, he made a forward motion with one hand. Once more, the coffle of slaves began trudging toward the harbor.

Kuda watched the Weasel melt back into the crowd, his face betraying nothing. Hefting the thick chains with which he was draped he began shuffling forward once again. Although aware that none returned from the galleys, he walked with shoulders squared and head held high. That morning, he had awoken from a drugged slumber in an iron cage, surrounded by a motley collection of condemned men. The men were loudly bemoaning their circumstances and speculating as to the fate that awaited them. Kuda had remained silent. The cages occupants had given the brooding barbarian a wide berth. It wasn't long before the guards arrived to drag them out, one by one, and put them in manacles. Now, reaching the end of the street, the group emerged onto a quayside where they came to a clanking halt.

✝

Heading for the wharf where the prisoners waited, the Imperial trireme steered a straight course across the wide harbor, ignoring the bustling vessels around it as a hunting wolf would shun yapping domestic pets. The warship was long, narrow, low in the water and designed for speed and quick maneuvers. Below the bow, fixed to the keel and projecting forward under the water-line, was the ram, a device of solid wood, reinforced and armed with iron. In action, the device could be used to devastating effect by stoving in the hulls of enemy vessels.One great square sail hung from a mast set a little forward of midship, but the vessel's main propulsion was provided by her long oars; sixty on each side of the hull. The hundred and twenty oaken blades, kept white and shining with pumice and the constant wash of the waves, rose and fell as if operated by the same hand, driving the galley forward at a prodigious speed.

So rapidly did she come on, the guardsmen in charge of the prisoners stepped back from the edge of the quay, alarmed. A man standing by the prow, raised his hand. At the signal, all oars flew up, poised a moment in the air, then fell straight down. The water boiled and bubbled about the oar blades, the trireme shook in every timber and immediately came to a halt. Another gesture of the hand, and the oars rose again, feathered, then fell. Those on the right, dropping toward the stern, pushed forward, while those on the left, dropping toward the bow, pulled backward. The oars pulled and pushed against each other to swing the ship on its axis until it settled gently broadside onto the wharf.

The movement brought the stern into view. On its raised platform, the helmsman sat with his hand upon the long tiller. A trumpet was blown, brief and shrill. From the hatchways poured the marines, all in superb equipment, brazen helms, burnished shields and javelins. They formed up in shining, ordered ranks by the bulwarks. When the oars touched the quayside, the gangway was lowered.

SHADOW OF THE BARBARIAN

✝

The prisoners were marched up the gangplank, which bounced and flexed under their weight. On reaching the deck, they were given into the charge of the overseer. He was an apish man, squat and broad-shouldered, with a face seamed by countless squalls. Wisps of dirty brown hair hung from under the iron helm that was pulled low over his forehead. His features were flat and hard, his teeth crooked and stained. He carried a rawhide whip on a thong from his wrist. Now and then, for no apparent reason, he flicked the tapered end against the bare legs of one of the men filing past him. It was a casual act, born of disinterest and disdain rather than calculated cruelty. Though each stroke was feathery light, it stung like a hornet and the victim gasped and skipped, shooting across the deck and down the waiting hatch with alacrity.

Kuda drew level with him. The overseer's lips drew back from his yellow teeth as he smiled widely. A bad one, he knew instinctively. He would have to watch him to make sure he didn't get out of hand.

"Hurry up!" he ordered. The lash popped as it lashed around Kuda's leg. The Northman stopped dead and turned his head slowly to stare into the overseer's muddy eyes.

"Yes!" the thick-set man encouraged him softly. For the first time, there was a sparkle of interest in his eyes. He altered his stance subtly, coming onto the balls of his feet.

"Yes!" he repeated. He wanted to take this big bastard, here, in front of all the others. They were going to live out the remainder of their short lives below these decks. Hot, thirsty days, during which tempers would be rubbed raw. He always liked to do it right at the beginning of a voyage. It only needed one, and it would save a lot of trouble later if he made an example right here above decks. That way, all of them would know what to expect if they started anything. In his experience, they never did start anything after that.

"Come on, outlander," he hissed. He enjoyed this part of his work, and he was very good at it. This cocky bastard would not be fit to row when he had finished with him. He wouldn't be much use to anybody with four or five ribs stoved in, and perhaps a broken jaw.

Kuda was too quick for him, though. He went down the hatch in a clattering rush, leaving the overseer braced and poised for his attack. Kuda's move took him completely off balance. By the time he aimed a hard cut of the lash at the Northman's legs, he was too late by a full half second. The stroke hissed and died in the air.

✝

The moon was four days from full. The hills loomed dark and mysterious over the beach, their gullies and bluffs touched with silver. Wrapped in a dark cloak Belsar sat in the stern sheets, one hand on the tiller, peering forward over the heads of the rowers. Twelve hand-picked crewmen worked the oars. All were armed.Nervously, he fingered the hilt of the broad-bladed cutlass he carried under his cloak. Belsar disliked these clandestine meetings, but the Weasel had sent an urgent demand for a rendezvous. He could not refuse such a request. The crew, who had been starved of plunder lately, were growing restless, and they valued the Weasel's information.

They came into the beach on one of the big swells, hissing over the sands on the foaming crest. As the waves began to retreat, the rowers jumped out and dragged the longboat high and dry.

"Keep the men under your eye, boatswain. Don't let them sneak away to look for drink and women," he warned the tattooed pirate. "We may be in a hurry when we return."

Motioning for two burly corsairs to follow him, he set off. They trudged together through the soft beach sand. Finding a path through the trees, they followed it. When they glimpsed the ruins of a temple up ahead, they slowed their pace and drew their weapons, approaching warily. The roof had collapsed long ago, leaving four bare walls and two dark windows that watched their approach like empty eye sockets.

Behind the windows, a light flared. The pirates froze, weapons raised. An unmistakably female figure appeared in the doorway, etched by the feeble light of a single torch.

"Put out that torch!" the captain snapped.

"Peace, Belsar. There is no-one within ten miles of this place," Ariane spoke soothingly.

Grunting, Belsar gestured his men forward. They pushed past Ariane to search the ruins.

Shrugging her shoulders, she approached the pirate captain.

"You have something for me?" he asked her.

"I have a message from Captain Kuda."

"No longer a captain," he said, teeth gleaming in his dark beard. "He is now lapdog to a Princess."

"I think not," she replied with a ghost of a smile. "Anyway, he wishes to meet with you to discuss a plan that will fill your holds with riches."

"Arrange it then!" he snarled in agitation. "You could have told me that by messenger. Why have you put me at risk by dragging me here?" He raised his cutlass, shooting glances at the surrounding foliage.

"There is a complication."

"There always is," he sighed, returning his gaze to her.

"Kuda has been sentenced to the galleys by the Princess's enemies."

"Pity," Belsar shook his head sorrowfully. "That's that then," he said, sheathing his cutlass. "What other news do you bring from the city?"

"The Emperor has gone mad and become a recluse," she began in a resigned voice. "The court, with no leadership, has turned into a snake pit of conspiracy. The guard are running amok claiming they are the sole repository of the Emperor's will. They are arresting or just plain murdering anyone who so much as blinks out of turn. The Emperor's new advisor, Shikrol, has gathered acolytes about him from less enlightened lands, and formed a new religion embracing the black arts. They are openly practicing sorcery, running around screaming heretic, planting spies and getting the guard to grab anyone who says a word against them. Every citizen arrested is sentenced to hard labor and put to work building some kind of shrine inside the Heronium Stadium. A place of human sacrifice whose first victim will be the Princess Semoon."

"It sounds bad," Belsar shrugged.

"Damn right it's bad. People are blaming Shikrol for everything. He seems to have the Emperor in his pocket."

Belsar looked skeptical. "I don't see how one single individual, no matter what weird abilities he has, can bring down a whole city. That's got to be pure paranoia."

Ariane nodded agreement. "Paranoia is at epidemic proportions right now."

"Well then, all in all, I'd say that Bansaray is a city best avoided. It's certainly not the place to be plunging recklessly into on some mad get-rich adventure." Belsar shrugged once again. "Like I said, it's a pity."

The two pirates returned from searching the ruins. "The place is deserted," one of them grunted.

"A pity indeed, to let a fortune slip through your fingers," Ariane spoke up in a loud, clear voice.

"What's this?" One of the men inclined his head toward the Weasel. "A fortune you say?" There was sharp interest in his voice.

Ariane turned toward the pirate. "Captain Kuda has come up with a scheme that will make every man aboard the *Shrike* as rich as a lord."

"Had a scheme you mean," Belsar cut in. "Whatever it was will die with him at the oars. Don't listen to her."

The *Shrike's* quartermaster, a grizzled man called Medak, chewed his lip. "Kuda has been sentenced to the galleys then. What vessel?"

"The *Revenge*," she answered without hesitation.

Belsar exploded a curse. "The *Revenge*! There you have it. That trireme is a pirate killer. She exists solely to hunt down buccaneers. She was in the vanguard of the fleet that destroyed the brotherhood of the coast just a few short weeks ago."

"She is alone now, scouring the Pelusian islands for stragglers from that battle," Ariane quickly informed them. "A bold captain could gather those stragglers together and attack the *Revenge* when she least expects it."

Medak nodded thoughtfully. "It could be done, but that would mean more shares. More risk, less return. What is this plan of Kuda's, anyway?"

"I know not. Kuda asked me to arrange a meeting with your captain to discuss it," she answered before glancing sideways at the scowling captain. "I do know that Kuda was sworn to protect Princess Semoon, and that she is now imprisoned and awaiting execution. If you were to aid him in freeing her, her gratitude would undoubtedly be boundless. What the Princess will allow you to take from the Imperial Treasury, even divided, will make you all rich beyond your dreams."

Medak and the other pirate exchanged glances, their eyes gleaming.

"What!" Belsar spluttered. "We barely escaped with our lives the last time we encountered the *Revenge* and now you fools are thinking of attacking her?"

"So, we ignore this chance and do what?" Medak retorted hotly. "Hide out in the Islands, waylaying fishermen. That's no life for a corsair! Kuda always had an eye for the main chance. If he says he can lead us to booty, I say we listen to him."

"I'm captain of the *Shrike*, Medak," Belsar hissed, his hand falling to his hilt. "You'd do well to remember that."

The pirates pivoted to face Belsar. Ariane took a few steps backward.

"You know the code," Medak raised his voice. "Every crewman has his say. We'll put it to the vote."

Belsar shifted his weight, taking up a fighting stance. He eyed the two burly corsairs, whose hands hovered over their sword hilts. Medak was getting on in years but the other pirate was as tall as he was, and almost as big. Leathery, lank and long-boned, he had a face like a fighting dog, hacked by fists and steel and a well-earned reputation as a killer. Slowly, Belsar moved his hand away from the hilt of his cutlass.

"Very well," he nodded. "I'm a reasonable man. We'll put it to the crew."

The two men grunted and, taking a wide berth around their captain, set off along the path back to the beach.

When they had gone, Belsar rounded on the Weasel. "You overstepped the mark there, bitch!" he growled.

Ariane met his glare openly, unflinching. She smiled with lips that were as red as a summer rose. "A girl has to earn her ten per cent," she said, her voice a low purr.

He took a step toward her then stopped when he saw the small crossbow she held in one hand. It was pointed straight at his gut. Her smile had disappeared.

"You had better get back to your ship while you are still Captain."

Grinding his teeth in anger, Belsar spun around and stamped off after his men.

✝

The Imperial trireme, *Revenge*, was skimming across the surface of the ocean. Below decks, stretching the entire length of the vessel, lay the great cabin. The cabin was the central compartment of the galley, lighted by three broad hatchways with a row of stanchions that ran from end to end, supporting the roof. With the hatchways open, the compartment had the appearance of a sky-lit hall.

At the after end of the cabin, several steps led up to a platform, where the overseer sat. From there, he could keep a watchful eye on the rowers. Before him was the sounding table, upon which the chief of the rowers beat time with a gavel. The rowers sat upon benches that were fixed to the ship's timbers at either side of a raised central walkway. Fixed to every bench was a chain with heavy anklets. Each oarsman was locked into an anklet with no chance of escape, even in the event of the ship sinking. If the ship floundered, the galley slaves, chained to their benches, would be left to die. Communication between the rowers was not allowed. Day after day, they bent to the oars without speaking. Short respites were given for sleep and the snatching of food.

Late one afternoon the men rested on their oars. Under the eyes of the overseer, two slaves wheeled a food barrow along the central walkway, handing a small wooden bowl of fish stew to each rower. When they reached Kuda's bench, the overseer shouldered the food-bearing slave aside and took the bowl from his hands. He served Kuda's portion himself.

"We must look after this Northlander," he said loudly. "We want him to be strong for his work at the oar." With that, he spooned an extra portion of fish into the bowl and offered it to Kuda.

"Here, bumpkin." As Kuda reached for the bowl, the overseer deliberately let it drop onto the floor. The hot stew splashed over Kuda's feet. The overseer stepped into the mess of fish guts and ground it under his boot. Then, gripping the rawhide whip with one hand, he stood back and grinned.

"Hey, you clumsy northern swine, you only get one ration. If you want to eat it off the deck, that's up to you."

He waited expectantly for Kuda to react. To his surprise and disappointment, the barbarian dropped his eyes, leaned forward and began to scrape the mashed fish into the bowl with his fingers before scooping a ball of it into his mouth and munching on it stolidly.

"You filthy barbarians will eat anything, even your own dung," he snarled and went on down the compartment.

As he walked away Kuda raised his head, his eyes locking onto the ring of keys the man carried on his belt.

†

In the deeper darkness that comes before dawn, the Imperial trireme lay anchored between the islands. Her streamlined hull motionless, but somehow charged with leaping speed. Up on deck, marines lay slumbering, their weapons close at hand, while sailors acting as sentries strained their eyes across the dark waters and muttered into their beards. They were uneasy with their captain's decision to anchor amongst the pirate infested islands but, equally, they knew it would have been folly to continue threading their way through the archipelago's treacherous shoals in darkness. So, with shoulders slumped in resignation, they kept watch. Below deck the rowers slept upon their oars or stretched out along the benches as much as their ankle-irons would allow. The overseer made his rounds every few hours, meticulously counting heads, even in the middle of the night. He stood over Kuda, deliberately shining the beam of his lantern into his face, waking him every time he passed down the deck.

The overseer never tired of his efforts to provoke the big Northerner. It had become a challenge, a contest between them. He knew it was there, he had seen it in the barbarian's eyes. Just a flash of the violence, menace and power, and he was determined to bring it out, flush it into the open where he could destroy it.

✝

Along both sides of the hull, the galley's oars lay at rest, their blades raised out of the water, the long shafts pulled inboard and secured. With barely a ripple, two sinewy arms reached up from the liquid darkness to catch hold of an oar blade. Corded muscles strained as a man hauled himself from the ocean to lay full length along an oar's wooden shaft. He paused thereto recover his breath, eyes sweeping the vessel's rail for any signs he'd been spotted. Satisfied, he fumbled at his waist and drew a nine-inch knife from his belt. Placing it between his teeth, he began shuffling along the oars shaft. On reaching the oar-hole, he carefully drew aside the flap of bull-hide and slid aboard.

He lay for a moment, spread-eagled beneath the rowing benches with his ears pricked. Hearing nothing but the snores of sleeping men, he began slithering forward on his belly. The crowded below decks stank like an animal cage. His mouth twisted in disgust as he squelched his way through human waste. The stench was ungodly. Holding his breath he scanned the rowers he was passing, looking for one in particular. He continued on, cursing under his breath, until he saw the outline of the man he sought; a huge fellow with massively muscled arms. Thanking the Gods, he twisted in that direction.

Kuda was slumped over his oar feigning sleep when the intruder eased into view beneath him. He glared balefully down at the man who now lay between his feet, looking up at him.

"You are not surprised to see me, Captain?" the man whispered.

"I heard you coming five minutes ago, Maltho, you rogue," Kuda replied in a low voice. "So, the Weasel got my message to Belsar."

"She did, and I am here to free you," grinned the filth mired buccaneer.

"How do you plan to do that?"

"With this." He flourished his knife. "I'll hack free the staple that anchors the chain."

Kuda frowned. "Too much noise. Anyway, the overseer will be making his rounds again shortly. I have a better way. Give me your knife," he grinned mirthlessly. "I have a debt to repay before I leave."

The overseer moved slowly along the raised central walkway, directing the light of his lantern over the sleeping rowers. He stopped in front of Kuda again.

"I know you are awake, barbarian," he rasped.

Kuda lifted his chin and stared at him.

"I'll tell you something now, you great oaf," the man grinned wolfishly. "I don't like you. You're trouble, and my task aboard this ship is to prevent trouble. The best way to do that is to stop it before it starts." He fingered the club at his belt, fourteen inches of hard wood, the end drilled and filled with lead. He could break bone with it, crush in a skull to kill a man instantly if he needed to, or, with a delicate alteration of the weight of the blow, merely stun him. He was an artist with the club, as he was with the whip. "You will not survive this voyage outlander scum. I guarantee you that."

Slowly, Kuda leaned back from the oar he had been resting on to reveal the nine inches of gleaming steel he held in his fist.

Terror filled the overseer's piggy eyes. "Where …?" He backpedaled, dropping the lantern, his hand clawing at the club. Behind him, a shadow rose from between the benches to slap a filthy hand over his mouth.

Kuda sprang to the length of his chains. The knife darted out with surgical precision, its keen edge ripping through the man's fat throat. Gouts of blood washed over the blade as Kuda's tormentor dropped to the deck, gurgling his life away.

Stooping quickly, Maltho snatched the ring of keys from the overseer's belt. Sorting through them he bent quickly to the Northman's manacles. Disturbed by the noise, the men around them were raising their sleepy heads.

The manacles clattered to the deck. Kuda leapt up onto the central walkway. "Where is the *Shrike*?"

"The other side of the islands," answered the pirate. "There is a longboat waiting three cable lengths off the port beam. We can swim to her."

"You can swim. I mean to take this ship," he said, his face a grim mask of determination.

Maltho stared at him, goggle-eyed. "How can you do that? You are one man."

They both looked up when their ears detected muffled noises overhead; the marines were stirring.

"Best escape while you can, Maltho. Free as many of the slaves as you can, then leave the same way you came." He clapped a big hand on the wiry man's shoulder. "Now go with my thanks."

Without another word, Maltho whirled away to jump down amongst the benches and begin working with the keys.

Footsteps sounded on the wooden after stairs that led down from the deck above. "What's going on?" a stern voice demanded.

Kuda took hold of the end of his oar. Yanking it from its resting position he jammed the length of oak between the benches and heaved back. The wood began to bend. All around him, freed slaves were rising out of the shadows, shaking off their chains. Naked except for cinctures about their loins, the men's bodies were a mass of whip-scarred muscle, their eyes gleaming pools of malice.

"Marines! Marines! To arms," bellowed the voice from the stairs.

Kuda exerted his strength on the oar, which bent almost to breaking point. Ropes of muscle writhed beneath his sweat drenched skin as, with one final explosive grunt of effort, the wooden shaft snapped. He staggered back, holding a long thick length of oak. The oars were loaded with lead in the handles, and that made for a formidable weapon. Turning quickly, he saw marines cautiously descending the stairs their shields held high, spears leveled, helmeted heads tucked in behind.

He looked around him at the gathered slaves. "You want to be free men again?" he roared. "Follow me!"

The response was a loud chorus of wild yells. Without waiting to see if anyone followed him, Kuda rushed at the armored men bellowing like a madman. He swung the length of oak in a long, looping blow. It hummed faintly over his head as he brought it down on a shield. The force of the blow smashed a marine off his feet and sent him spinning into the benches. The long spears reached out, lunging and stabbing at him. Swinging the length of weighted oak like a scythe, he advanced, buckling shields and breaking limbs. Just then, the slaves charged past him, swinging heavy chains and shouting defiance to add their weight to the melee.

The marines were forced back up the stairs. Kuda drove forward, trampling their bodies under his bare feet as the splintered oar rose and fell. Stooping quickly, he snatched up a fallen short sword and dropping the wood went to work.

†

The fight was going badly for the marines. Hardy though they were, and fierce and fully armed, they still could not match the snarling savagery of the freed slaves who'd set upon them. Their officer bellowed orders at them from the top of the stairs, but still the marines retreated. Kuda grabbed the shoulder of a burly slave and spun him around.

"Take half the men and get forward, use the hatch there to reach the upper deck," he shouted into the man's face. "There are weapons stacked around the base of the mast ready for instant use, axes spears and javelins. Take them and fall on the marines from behind. Go!"

Shoving the man away, he plunged back into the fight.

†

Maltho wriggled through the oar-hole and dropped into the dark ocean. Spluttering to the surface, he struck out in the direction he knew the longboat would be waiting. The sounds of battle receded behind him as he ploughed through the water. Dawn was breaking and up ahead in the faint grey light, a boat crammed to the gunwales with armed men began to coalesce out of the gloom.

Treading water, he waved his arms in the air. There was sudden movement aboard the boat and oars slid into the water. The longboat eased alongside him and hands reached down to pull him on board. Sprawled between the benches, he gasped for breath, looking up at the circle of hard faces that stared questioningly down at him.

"Where is Captain Kuda?" one of them hissed impatiently.

"Captain Kuda has taken leave of his sanity," Maltho rasped. "He is leading the galley slaves against the marines. He means to take the *Revenge* for himself!"

The questioner's pockmarked face became a picture of incredulity.

✝

Kuda glared at the shield wall that stretched from gunwale to gunwale across the entire width of the ship. His barrel chest heaved. His hair hung in lank strands about his shoulders. Blood streamed from dozens of lacerations, mixing with spatters of grime and gore. Carried along by their naked ferocity, the desperate band of slaves had gained the upper deck, only to have their headlong charge abruptly halted by an unbroken line of touching shields and leveled spears. The marines training and discipline had asserted itself. The freed men who had boiled out of the hatchway now found themselves trapped between the raised, easily defended afterdeck packed with sailors who had rallied around their captain and the impregnable wall of shields.

The slaves milled about, casting uncertain glances at the giant, panting barbarian, who, having freed them from cruelty and deprivation, now stood unmoving in their midst. Close by him a slave was lifted off his feet and slammed to the deck by a crossbow bolt. The sailors on the afterdeck had armed themselves with these deadly weapons and were putting them to good use. Kuda stooped to a fallen shield and thrust his left arm through its loops. Standing upright again, he continued to glower at the shield wall, waiting.

Then it happened. The slaves from the forward hatch fell upon the marines from behind. Kuda heard their wild screaming and saw the line of armored men shudder under the unexpected onslaught. The disciplined line became disordered and gaps appeared between shields. Kuda knew the gaps were only fleeting. Within moments, the slaves would be beaten back and order restored, allowing the marines to form up again. This, then, was the moment on which the outcome of the battle, the rescue of the Princess, the restoration of an enlightened people and a Northern barbarian's promise to a terrified girl, rested.

None of this passed through Kuda's mind, though. He only saw the gaps. Hefting his shield, he roared a battle cry before launching himself forward. Without pausing, he swept aside two spears with the shield and hurled his body at a weak spot in the wall. The shields parted under the impetus of his charge and he plunged deeper into the packed ranks, his sword chopping right and left, crunching through armor with terrible force. A wedge of newly armed slaves pushed in behind him, spitting their hate. The wedge split the shield wall apart. Kuda thrust beneath a shield and felt his blade slide into a man's thigh, he twisted and ripped the blade free. Turning, he dodged a sword that flickered toward his throat. Seeing that his attacker had lost his helmet, Kuda smiled and butted the man on the bridge of his nose. He staggered back to fall under the grunting shoving mass of men. Kuda looked around him. The marines had failed to hold the line. Assaulted from two sides, they were being forced back against the ships rails. Yet even though they were losing the disciplined troops fought on. It was a bitter struggle. The freed slaves were in no mood to take prisoners, and the battle spread to form knots of fighting men who shouted and screamed at one another.

Crossbows cracked and hissed, bolts thumped into flesh as the sailors on the afterdeck picked their targets. The battle wasn't won yet, Kuda realized.Lifting his battered shield, he bellowed at the men around him. "To me! To me! Let's finish this." He leveled his short sword, red from hilt to tip, at the men on the afterdeck. Teeth gritted, shield held high, he dashed toward them. Deadly shafts whistled and buzzed around him. One of the bolts struck his shield, numbing his arm. All around him slaves were being plucked backward in sprays of blood. The charge faltered as men sought cover from the lethal missiles. Kuda pounded on alone, a red mist before his eyes.

The fusillade of bolts faltered and then stopped. Kuda slithered to a halt before the barricaded steps that led up to the afterdeck. Looking up, he saw howling pirates swarming over the stern rail to fall upon the hapless sailors. Maltho had apparently persuaded the longboat full of cut-throats to lend a hand. Cutlasses rose and fell amongst the sailors, who flung down their weapons and pleaded for mercy. The sea-wolves, knowing the value of experienced sailors, granted it. Maltho pushed forward to the rail. He stared down at Kuda and, with the hint of a smile hovering on his blood-spattered face, shouted out, "The ship is yours, Captain."

†

The white sand beach shone like a snowfield under the blazing sun, reminding Kuda fleetingly of his Northern homeland. Though the illusion was quickly dispelled by the steaming heat and the tropical vegetation fringing the beach, it nevertheless triggered a longing for the honest freshness of an icy wind.

SHADOW OF THE BARBARIAN

He squatted on his heels upon the sands, sweating under the shade of a stretched canvas awning that did nothing to prevent the sticky atmosphere pressing in upon him. It was much worse for the armed and armored men who were gathered behind him under the full glare of the sun. But, he reasoned, the hardened ex-slaves were inured to such a mild discomfort. Shading his eyes with one hand, he looked out to sea at the two vessels rocking lazily at their anchors. The sleek *Revenge* and the newly arrived *Shrike*. Squinting, he surveyed the longboats sliding up onto the shelving beach, inspecting the men who leapt ashore from them.

Even weary, sweat stained and dirty from their recent misfortunes, the pirates presented a wild and crudely romantic image. Determined to make an impression before the former slaves, they came ashore with the swagger of an invading army, strutting in their sea boots as though they owned the island. Hard, watchful eyes peered from beneath the drooping brims of their wide hats. Heavy cutlasses and curved knives hung from their wide, decorated leather belts. The weapons were in easy reach, an unarguable back-up to each man's buccaneer bravado. Like most sea rovers, a pirate's wealth was ostentatiously displayed on his person. Jewelry glittered. Gold seemed to be a particular favorite. It hung from their ears in heavy loops, around necks in chains or medallions, it decorated the hilts of knives, flashed in their grins and weighted down hands and arms in the form of rings and bracelets.

The sea-wolves came from no particular tribe or nation. Their weather-beaten, often scarred faces ranged from deep mahogany to blue black. There were equine faces with high foreheads and prominent noses, there were broad, flat-featured faces with slanting, almond eyes. Pirate crews came from all over the world. What held them together was greed and the hardship of their chosen life, coupled with a fierce pride in their freedom and individualism.

It was Belsar, dressed in all his finery, who led them up the beach to where Kuda waited. They came to a halt just before the awning. For a long moment, the two groups stood, glaring sullenly at each other. Belsar broke the heavy silence. "Kuda, Kuda." He shook his head ruefully. "You never cease to amaze me. The last time we met, you were in the company of a beautiful Princess. This time, you are captain of a beautiful trireme."

"May I never cease to amaze you, my friend," said Kuda, stepping forward. The men gripped wrists in the warrior's greeting.

"Wine?" he indicated the table and two chairs that had been set up beneath the canopy. The furniture had been brought ashore from the *Revenge*, along with a flagon of her former Captain's wine.

Belsar nodded. Sweeping his wide brimmed hat from his head, he took the offered seat in the shade. Kuda poured two goblets of wine before settling into the opposite seat. After taking a long slurp, Belsar lowered the goblet and wiped the back of his hand across his lips. He nodded appreciatively. "A fine wine. The *Revenge's* previous Captain lived well it seems."

"Not anymore," Kuda grunted.

"Ah, yes. I take it that is him dangling by his neck from your yard arm."

"It is. My men could not be restrained. They slaughtered everybody they could lay hands on."

"Really!" Belsar eyed the desperate-looking band gathered behind Kuda. "I take it they have calmed down somewhat since then?"

"They've never been happier."

Belsar leaned closer to begin speaking with the low-voiced urgency of a practiced conspirator. "Whereas my crew have never been unhappier. By all the God's, Kuda, if you have a scheme to make us all rich, then it had better be a good one."

Grinning suddenly, his teeth a brilliant white against his sun-darkened skin, Kuda rose to his feet. "Men! This is the luckiest day of your lives," he boomed. "Gather round and let me tell you of the heaps of gold and jewels that will soon be yours. Riches beyond measure!"

Belsar buried his head in his hands and groaned.

SEVEN

The Heronium Stadium was immense. The multitude that had gathered there for the opening day of the summer games was easily accommodated within its soaring circular walls. Traditionally, this was a time of celebration; but not this year. This year, a definite sense of unease rippled around the tiers of seating overlooking the broad circular amphitheater of sand. A hundred thousand citizens stared in mute dread at the stadium's newly constructed centerpiece. It was an extraordinary structure. Rising like a small mountain from the flatness of the amphitheater floor, layers of huge, well-cut, masonry blocks were piled high, heaped almost haphazardly, one upon the other. With no doors or windows, the construction squatted in the middle of the broad, circular space like a giant tombstone. It was featureless except for a pathway that wound around its great stone bulk from base to summit, just wide enough for three men to walk abreast. The winding path debouched onto the structure's flat top, which was level with the surrounding tiers of seats.The summit was bare but for a flat slab of stone carved all over with runes. It occupied the center of the open space like an altar.

Massive bronze doors broke the circle of the amphitheater's otherwise featureless wall. Above the doors was a lavishly decorated balcony, where the Emperor sat on his imperial throne, unmoving, his body hunched over, his eyes staring into space. The young man's sallow features bore the stamp of the hidden parasite that clung to his back. He had spider veins on his cheeks and dark circles beneath his eyes that not even the thickest of cosmetics could hide.

The heavy doors below the balcony swung open. The crowd seemed to hold its breath. A drum could be heard, slow and steady as a heartbeat. Figures began shuffling slowly out through the bronze portals, a double file of black-robed and hooded figures. They were followed by rank after rank of soldiers in eye-hurting polished armor, spears in hand and shields on their arms.Then came Princess Semoon, hemmed in by burly guardsmen. Dressed in a simple white robe, her hair a glossy dark cascade that hung to her waist, she held her head high, her expression one of total despair. There was a rope tied around her neck, and when she stumbled, a guard yanked on it to jerk her back to her feet. A groan of disapproval went up around the stadium at this display, though it was ignored by the guards, who marched stolidly on. Following behind the armored men came more black-robed acolytes, their shaven heads bared, their mouths moving, repeating the same phrases over and over again. A ritual chant that rose and fell. There was a dirge of death to the sound; the wailing of the dead.

✝

Oars moving in unison, the *Revenge* sped across the bay, heading toward the wide mouth of a river, her course bypassing the city of Bansaray and its harbor with its tangled mass of shipping. The former galley slaves pulled with a will, singing over the oars, their high spirits abounding, their arms and backs indefatigable.Kuda moved along the crowded deck, striding amongst pirates and former slaves, not with the aloofness of a Captain, but as a man. He stopped along the way to share a joke or to give a greeting. He laughed and the buccaneers laughed with him. Kuda was a man they could follow. Not a man who would command them from the afterdeck, but a corsair like themselves. A man who would fight, bleed and even die with them.

He joined Belsar at the steering oar just as they were entering the broad river mouth. The pirate looked enquiringly at the Northman.

"Are you ready to share any more of the details of your plan with me?"

Kuda nodded, his expression grim. "The Heronium Stadium abuts the river, does it not?"

"It does," Belsar answered with a frown. "But its walls rise sheer out of the water. They're high, very high. An assault from the river is unthinkable. We don't have enough men and the Princess does not have enough time. The sacrificial ceremony will have already begun."

"Get us upriver to a point opposite the stadium, from there, all will become clear," Kuda said. Squaring his jaw, he added. "Trust me."

Belsar grinned without humor. "I hope you know what we're doing."

†

With solemn dignity, the procession reached the base of the great mound of limestone blocks and began a slow ascent. Behind them, the bronze doors boomed shut as the files of somber figures climbed unhurriedly around the winding path to emerge onto the flat stone-flagged summit. On the far side of the crude altar stone, a solitary black-robed figure stood waiting for them. Eyes glinting with triumph, Shikrol smiled his ghastly smile. At a barked order, the guardsmen hurried to take up position around the edge of the flagged area. Facing the crowd, they held their weapons ready, forming a hedge of spears that ringed the flattened summit.

Semoon was dragged forward, toward the slab of rune-encrusted black stone. She fought down a sudden rush of despair when rough hands tore the white robe from her body. In her nakedness, she still stood proud, though she averted her eyes from Shikrol's malevolent gaze. It was at that moment that she finally realized that Kuda had failed her. The last shred of hope shriveled within her breast when robed acolytes grabbed at her. Pushing and pulling, they drew her out on the altar, clamping her legs and arms into the manacles that waited there. A roar rose from one hundred thousand throats, compounded of anger and dismay. Shikrol could feel the rise of the mob's emotions and, at its peak, he raised his arms and began intoning words not uttered in a millennia.The words of the summoning.

✝

As the mob's wail of despair erupted from the stadium opposite them Kuda's head jerked around, his eyes blazing.

"We're too late," Belsar shook his head sorrowfully.

Kuda leapt to the steering sweep and, pushing the helmsman aside, heaved upon the long tiller. The ship heeled over hard, cutting across the broad river's current. He strained and heaved and, with a muscle cracking effort, turned the vessel so that her sharp prow pointed toward the far bank and the rearing cliff-like walls of the colosseum.

Eyes flashing in anger, Belsar roared. "What are you doing? You'll have us aground!"

"There, there. We go there," Kuda snarled through gritted teeth, jutting his chin toward the far bank. "Tell the rowers to double up and pull until their backs break. Do it, now!"

Still not fully comprehending, Belsar blinked up at the smooth walls of honey-colored stone that rose from the river's far bank. That's when he saw it. A moan of disbelief escaped his lips.

The re-enactment of sea battles had always been popular with the mob, and Heronium Stadium had been designed to facilitate such displays. River water could be let into the stadium through sluices, turning the amphitheater into a lake. Once the lake's water level equalized with that of the river outside, a larger wooden gate would be opened to allow half-sized galleys and triremes to enter through a short canal and do battle. When the battle was over and the gates sealed, the water could be quickly drained away via underground channels.

Belsar pointed a quivering finger at the wooden gate, the only break in the palisade of towering walls. "You don't mean …"

Kuda cut him off with a burst of anger. "If I had told you earlier, would any of you have joined me? We're here now, and there is no other way." Bulges of iron muscle writhed beneath Kuda's skin as the long sweep bent almost to breaking point under his hands. "The rowers, you fat bastard!" he gasped. "Go tell the rowers. Ramming speed!"

†

Out of the clear blue sky, roiling and bunching over the stadium, thick dark clouds appeared. The temperature began to drop. With it, the mutterings of the mob dwindled down to be replaced by a definite air of foreboding. Shikrol's hatchet face became more wild-eyed and animated as he continued to spit his obscene ritual at the sky. Tears sparkling on her cheeks, Semoon twisted and writhed upon the cold stone. Excited acolytes pressed in on all sides. Suddenly, the heavy gate holding back the river trembled under a heavy impact.

†

"Backwater! Backwater!" Kuda yelled fiercely. Handing the steering oar back to the helmsman he leapt down from the raised stern to sprint along the deck, roaring orders as he went. "Arm yourselves! Prepare for battle!"

Belsar raised his eyes in a silent prayer before stooping to bark orders down the hatchway. The pace man in charge of the rowers beat a swift cadence upon the sounding table and the long sweeps reversed their blades.

Kuda slid to a halt at the prow, his sharp eyes scanning the iron bound gate. He grunted in satisfaction when he saw fresh scarring where the baulks of heavy timber had split. Calculating the growing distance between the armored ram at the bow and the splintered gate, he came to a decision. Whirling around to look back down the length of the deck, which resembled a disturbed ants' nest with the men milling about and calling to each other enthusiastically, he caught Belsar's eye and swept his arm forward.

Belsar nodded and bellowed an instruction down to the man at the sounding board. Blades reversing again, the oars dipped. Responding to the sounding board, the rowers reached forward full length, and, deepening the dip of their oars, pulled suddenly with all their united force, bending all their strength to the long sweeps. The galley, quivering in every timber, answered with a leap as the oars dug in along her flanks.

Kuda looked down at the bow wave that spread back from the armored beak in a sharp arrowhead of ripples. The trireme was moving as swiftly as a horse at full gallop, its banks of oars sending up a white spray as it sheared through the water. The stroke boomed out below decks, the pulse of it coming throbbing up through the planking beneath his feet. He raised his eyes to the sturdy gate that rushed toward him.

✝

With terrible slowness, Shikrol slid a wickedly curved knife from the voluminous sleeve of his robe and raised it high above the prostrate woman upon the altar. The crowd seemed to hold its breath as, with infinite care, he lowered the obsidian blade and ran its razored edge along the struggling princess's flank. A long cut opened up in the woman's creamy white flesh. Ruby red blood oozed from the gash to run in rivulets across the black stone. At that moment, lightning split the sky and the runes carved into the stone slab began to glow with an internal hellfire. Fierce winds sprang from nowhere to whistle around the walls, shrieking sibilantly. It grew darker, a strange, unnatural darkness, as though some sinister, invisible force was soaking up all the light in the city. Shikrol threw back his head and howled like a madman. Around him, the air groaned like a living thing and the river gate exploded inward.

✝

There was a massive impact followed by a grinding, crackling uproar of bursting timber. Kuda was almost catapulted from the prow, but he hung on with legs and arms braced. The river burst through the disintegrating wood, taking the *Revenge* with it. The slim galley entered the narrow canal in a gut-swooping rush, carried upon the wildly plunging crest of a huge wave. Oar-tips brushed the stone walls and the oars were dashed from the hands of the rowers and the rowers from their benches. People were screaming in panic. Jaw clenched, Kuda clung to the bow like a grim figurehead, his eyes slitted his black hair streaming behind him from the speed of the trireme's passage. The *Revenge* dropped twenty feet into the boil and surge of water that was sweeping around the amphitheater. She began swinging on her axis, rocking from side to side in the turbulent water. Clinging on, the men blinked and gaped at the scene they had come upon so suddenly. They found themselves within a circular lagoon rimmed by a stone wall, beyond which rose serried rows of packed seating. In the center of the lagoon, almost filling it, was an island of piled stone. The stone made the lagoon seem like a moat of water surrounding it.

While the water still churned and creamed about the hull, Kuda turned to bellow down the long deck where the men were clutching for balance at the nearest support.

"Never has a ship been so well named," he roared. Heads jerked around toward him. "For 'revenge' is what we're here for. Bloody revenge against those that have enslaved us, burned our galleys and tortured and killed our comrades." Kuda's eyes flashed as they swept over the crew. Their attention was totally focused on him now. "Victims no more! This is our time! Our moment! Our revenge!" He made a chopping motion with his arm toward the figures who were clustered thickly on the newly formed island. "Take it to them!" he bellowed. With that, the men stirred and growled like hunting hounds on the leash. Then the helm was put over.

†

There are some things that are unbelievable. Even when they are seen to happen, they cannot be accepted. The crowd knew they were witnessing something they would tell their grandchildren about and they would tell their children and there would be no end to the telling. So, despite their growing fears, they remained rooted to their seats, hypnotized by the spectacle playing out before them.

†

The sky was dark as dusk now, the gusting wind sending waves before it across the water. Kuda stood on the *Revenge's* deck swinging a boarding grapnel around his head in long swooping revolutions. He hurled it outwards, the line snaking out behind. The iron hook skidded across the island's cut stone blocks, but when Kuda jerked it back, it lodged firmly in a gap of well-dressed limestone. One of the island's men-at-arms ran forward and raised a sword to cut it free. An archer at the masthead drew the fletching of an arrow to his lips and loosed. The arrowhead buried itself in the man's throat. Dropping the sword, he clutched at the shaft as he staggered backward and collapsed.

The successful grapnel was followed by a score of others. In moments, the *Revenge* was bound to the island by a spider's web of sturdy ropes. Too many for the island's defenders to sever. Brawny pirates heaved upon the lines, closing the gap between island and ship quickly. Kuda ducked down behind the gunwale as a swarm of crossbow bolts slashed down from the island's summit, the deadly missiles thumping harmlessly into the vessel's sides. Vaulting over the gunwale, the Northman reached over his shoulder to draw his saber from the sheath that hung down his back. A cacophony of war-like yells rose behind him as the mixed crew of buccaneers and freed slaves poured onto the island to exact their bloody vengeance.

Screaming like avenging furies, the triremes raiding-force scrambled up the stone blocks, to be met at the island's flat top by the braced shields of the palace guardsmen. The two groups smashed into each other in a grinding of flesh and bone, underscored by the crunch of chopping blades and the screams of the dying. The enemy's ranks thickened as more guardsmen rushed across the summit to meet the charge. The two throngs of men were locked together until Kuda ploughed straight into the heart of the fight. The massive Northman roared and struck from side to side, scattering men in sprays of crimson gore. Spears thrust at him, but he swept them contemptuously aside. The spears were proving to be useless at such close quarters so, almost as one, the disciplined guard dropped them and drew their swords. The swords flickered like lightning, crashing on shields and helmets, rasping blade to blade. Kuda ducked a swinging blade, before stabbing the man in his armpit. He pushed forward, trampling bodies as his bloody saber rose and fell. He swayed back to let the tip of a sword whistle past his nose. Giving his attacker no time to recover, his saber tip flicked out to rip the man's throat open. Great gouts of blood splashed across the stones, which were becoming slick underfoot. He plunged on. Suddenly, the path was clear before him. Glancing back, he saw the bloody trail he had hewed through the crush of his enemies. All along the line, the ranks of guardsmen were slowly being forced to give ground under the onslaught.

His saber, notched and bloodied, quivered in his grip as he glared ahead. Looking across the flat space toward the altar stone, his eyes found the skull-faced sorcerer, his head tilted back, screaming incantations to the driven clouds in an alien language. All the while, he held a black-bladed knife poised over the squirming form of the Princess. He saw the deep cuts in Semoon's pale body and the snakes of scarlet blood running down the sides of the stone. Deep thunder rumbled overhead, vibrating the flagged-stones beneath his feet. Terrific winds tore viciously at him. Overhead, shadowy forms flapped at the edges of his vision, making the hairs on the back of his neck rise. The air seemed to be charged with evil.

Snarling wordlessly, he lunged forward to be met by a swarm of dark-robed acolytes wielding long, glittering knives. He grinned ruthlessly, blind rage and hatred etched onto his broad features. Blood spattered into the wind as his saber wove a web of death about him. A fanatical gleam lit the acolyte's dark eyes. Frothing lips hurled curses. A knife blade scored the flesh of his forearm. Yet, the seething mass fell back before the enraged barbarian, who pushed inexorably forward over a carpet of tangled bodies.

Kuda's arm shot out over the slab of black stone. Catching Shikrol by the throat his fingers dug into the necromancer's soft flesh like steel bands. Incantation cut off in mid-flow, the sorcerer gave a strangled cry as he was lifted off his feet. Spitting their fury, the acolytes rushed at the barbarian again. Shaking the sorcerer like a rat, he threw Shikrol at the screaming madmen and leapt up onto the broad flat stone. Standing astride the Princess like a bronzed colossus he hacked right and left, parting heads from bodies in plumes of blood. The acolyte's screaming was almost bestial; no words could be heard, only their hate could be felt. Like the angry shrieking of some inchoate monster. Claw-like hands reached for him, only to be severed at the wrist by his flashing blade. One of their number gained the top of the slab to be disemboweled by a lightning backhand slash. Tripping on the coils of his own entrails, he fell back into the rampaging mass. Kuda's crew broke through and charged toward the altar, their whirling blades stabbing, cutting and slicing into the pack of rabid priests.

Dropping to his knees beside Semoon, Kuda cuffed the gore from his eyes and stooped over her.

"Semoon, Semoon! Are you alive girl?"

Through a haze of pain, she looked up, her gaze fixing on him. "I knew you'd come ..." she lied, letting out a heart-wrenching sob.

"Of course," he grunted. "I gave you my word."

Laying down his saber, he turned to the fetters that bound her. "Let's get you out of here." Clumsily, his fingers began pulling at the pins holding her manacles closed. With effort, they fell away. He dragged her to her feet and held her against him until her knees grew steady. She held on to him, sobbing, weak from her wounds. Belsar came running up, breathing hard.

"Here, get her back to the *Revenge*," Kuda yelled, handing the Princess down to the sturdy pirate captain.

Belsar took her in his arms. "What about …?" The words died on his lips. He was staring wide-eyed at something beyond Kuda. Something horrible. Kuda felt an exhalation on his back. A coldness that carried with it the tang of the abyss.

†

The blood-soaked raiders began backing away, horror etched upon their features. An eerie quiet descended. The surviving acolytes prostrated themselves. Slowly, Kuda turned to see a slit of blackness expanding in the air. Something was seeping through it into this world. Something threatening, inexorable, and sentient. He felt the touch of eyes.

Hissing angrily, Shikrol appeared before the altar, his arms spread wide. Turning menacing eyes upon Kuda, he pointed and screamed. "This stone needs more blood!"

The barbarian quickly snatched up his blade. In a single, fluid movement, he swept the steel over and down in a humming arc, splitting the necromancer from crown to pelvis. Like a rotten fruit, the sorcerer burst open, splattering the altar's glowing runes with his bloody entrails.

In the few heartbeats it took Kuda to free his blade from the gripping carcass, a gateway opened behind him. Unimaginable distances and eons of time imploded into a singularity that could now be crossed, and something was crossing; something obscene. Abruptly and shockingly, a grey-green sac bulged and pulsed out of the black mouth. It was a small part of an immense body that still lay mostly hidden, iceberg like, in the abyss of blackness beyond the portal. Pushing back the fabric of earthly reality, the hideous form oozed forward, widening the gash between worlds.

The crew backed away, hunching over beneath the horror of the preternatural being that was splitting the sky above them.

"Sorcery."

The whispered word spread through the corsairs like an icy breath. Stolid and courageous as they were, every man amongst the raiding force harbored a deep-seated fear of the black arts. The word alone could loosen the bowels of the strongest amongst them. Kuda stood four square, using every measure of his will to hold down a rising dread and not yield to primitive panic. Fleshy, tentacular appendages whipped forward raking the air. Kuda recoiled, raising his blade to slash at the serpent-like lengths that sought to ensnare him. Across the entire width of the stadium, more tentacles lashed out, faster than the eye could follow, plucking victims from the crowds. Screams rang throughout the great bowl of the amphitheater as panic-stricken people began rushing toward the exits, trampling over one another in their terror. One of the bone-white cables wrapped itself about Semoon's waist, snatching her out of Belsar's grasp. Yelling and struggling, white limbs flailing, she was lifted high into the air.

Muscles, glossy with a pellucid dampness, churned and heaved to drag more of the horrors loathsome bulk through the gateway. Beyond that yawning black cavity, the furthest vacuums of immense space sucked in gales of wind. A grotesque head rotated into view, its jellied eyes focusing upon the lone barbarian, who stood his ground.

Beneath the eyes, a mucus-dripping, scarlet, membranous mouth puckered, presenting a ten-foot-wide circle of curved yellow teeth. Semoon shrieked in terror as she was lowered toward the toothy, viscous opening.

SHADOW OF THE BARBARIAN

From nowhere, a muscled tentacle coiled itself firmly around Kuda's ankle, sweeping him off his feet. He was swung around and up. Jumbled images flashed before his eyes; more tentacles curving in to drop helplessly shrieking victims into the revolting mouth. Dangling upside down he was also hoisted up over that salivating maw. A nauseating odor clogged his throat and smothered his lungs. It was the smell of rotting corpses, former victims of the creature's murderous appetite. With an explosive effort, he jerked upward and slashed his saber at the tentacle that held him. The blade sliced deep and the sinewy white flesh parted. Released, Kuda fell, landing on the soft, blubbery slope of the abomination's head. Unable to keep his footing on the gelatinous surface, he began an inexorable slide, head first, toward the slurping pit of the mouth. He cried out as his fingers slithered uselessly on the slimy flesh. Before his goggling eyes, bodies were being dropped into the twitching maw to be mangled by gnashing teeth. He saw Semoon's tentacle swing in and release her. With a long despairing wail she plummeted toward the churning horror. Gathering the steely muscles of his legs under him Kuda took off in a long leap that carried him out and over the pulsating hole. He grabbed at the falling Princess. Their bodies collided and his impetus carried them both across the mouth. On landing they bounced uncontrollably across soft, yielding flesh until he stabbed down hard with his saber. The steel sank deep into the vast body of foul matter, halting their slide and opening a long gash. A thick, oily fluid oozed out of the wound, and the stench of corruption became even stronger and more noisome. Thrusting his arms deep into the cut, Kuda violently pulled the flesh apart. The leprous tissue tore and the slit yawned. The great beast gave a shudder as its tentacles began seeking them. With one hand clamped to the hilt of his saber, Kuda wrapped his free arm around Semoon's waist and shoved her bodily into the tunnel of

97

living flesh he had created. Horror washed over him in sickening waves as he plunged in after her. The touch of the creature's flesh was so loathsome, Kuda's every nerve screamed out in revolt. The muscles of his jaw rippled as he clenched his teeth and squeezed deeper, pushing aside a terrified and gore-slick Semoon to get to work with his long blade.

✝

Belsar stood frozen in horror, his muscles locked in a terrifying paralysis. The tsunami of alien flesh swelled and grew before his disbelieving eyes, threatening to crush him with its great bulk. Long white serpents slashed the air above his head, snaking out to claim screaming victims. His panic was like an imprisoned animal raging. Then a jellied eye swiveled onto him and, under that baleful glare, something snapped. With a bloodcurdling shriek of hysterical fear, he turned and ran.

Leaping over prostrate acolytes and butchered bodies, fixing his gaze upon the trireme that bobbed at the island's rim, Belsar managed a turn of speed that would have impressed a young gazelle. All around him, friend and foe alike were fleeing, their battle forgotten in the face of this greater mind-numbing horror. Even the iron discipline of the guard had broken as they flung away their weapons and competed with the raiders to clamber aboard the already overloaded ship.

The sailors who had remained aboard the vessel were frantically chopping at the ropes that held the trireme fast. Others were heaving at the tiller to turn the galley away from the island, hoping to escape the nightmare that had erupted there. Without slowing his pace, Belsar leapt and gripped the gunwale with desperate, clutching fingers, pulling himself aboard.

"The oars! Get below and man the oars, you fools!" he roared breathlessly, beating at the panicked men that milled around him. "Pull till you burst your guts!"

The sweeps began working and the sleek warship pulled away from the island, out into the flooded amphitheater. Belsar shouldered his way to the afterdeck, glancing back to where the gigantic, veined, grey-green sweating monstrosity was looming over the stadium. He felt his sanity slipping away as he watched tentacles lashing out toward the ship to coil tightly around the trireme's hull. The entire ship was snared and hauled from the water to dangle in the air like a child's plaything. With despairing shrieks, some men flung themselves overboard, while others clung on in fear. Belsar managed to hang on, both physically and mentally, while all around him, madness reigned. No amount of riches were worth this he told himself as with an incoherent cry, he released his grip. Limbs flailing, he bounced across the slanting deck to tumble heavily over the rail.

The *Revenge* flexed and twisted in that deadly embrace until its hull could take no more. With a squeal of tortured timber, the galley shattered into pieces. The vessel's disintegration rained oars, men and wreckage across the amphitheater to dimple the water's surface.

✝

Kuda never ceased to strike, slashing repeatedly at the great bulk, widening the slit in its side. Somewhere deep inside his warrior brain, he had found the reserve of madness and energy he needed to carry him forward against the overwhelming horror. Teeth gritted, he fought against the clinging oleaginous embrace of the quivering flesh that pressed in upon him. As he dove down through layers of clinging tissue, his sleeveless tunic of linked mail was torn from his back. Clamping down on his revulsion, he burrowed on, deeper and deeper into the sponge-like consistency of the creature's flesh until, suddenly, he tore through into a larger space. Just enough light spilled past him to partly illuminate the dark void. Something was moving. Peering intently into the gloom, he could just make out the creature's glistening heart, pulsating convulsively within a web of writhing arteries. Ignoring the waves of nausea washing over him, he hefted his heavy blade in a two-handed grip and launched his body forward in a muscle-straining leap. The long steel plunged up to its hilt in the vile and loathsome organ. An alien shriek pounded his ears. All around him the living walls convulsed wildly. The monstrosity was hurt, badly hurt. A concussion crushed in upon him, his mind fragmented and he felt himself plummeting into a deep and dreadful pit.

EIGHT

It was the cold that hit Kuda first on regaining consciousness. He was very, very cold. He seemed to be laying in a pool of thick, oily fluid and he hurt all over, his body was a mass of weals, cuts and bruises. A dreadful stench permeated the air. Slowly, he sat up to look blearily about him. He was on the flagged top of the island, surrounded by piles of mangled bodies. The surface of the surrounding water was thick with corpses and wreckage. All around the arena, the circles of rising seats had been transformed into stepped heaps of the dead. Emptied of life, the stadium looked and felt like a monumental tomb.

A moan came to the Northman's ears from somewhere nearby. Pushing himself to his feet, he staggered toward the sound. Semoon's naked form lay face down, covered in the same foul-smelling ooze that covered him. She was stirring, so he helped her up. Focusing on him, her eyes flew wide open. Tossing back filth-matted hair she asked in a panicky voice, "Where is that thing?"

"Gone," he answered.

"Dead?"

"Probably. I stabbed it through the heart," he shrugged. "If such an abomination can be killed. In any event, the portal opened by that black-hearted sorcerer has closed. Dead or alive the demon is back where it came from."

She sagged against him, a large tear running down her face.

He pulled her close. "It's over, girl," he assured her.

She stayed like that for a moment before pulling away. A stricken look spread over her face. "My brother! We must seek out the Emperor without delay."

His brow furrowed. "Your wounds. You should get them ministered to. Can't it wait?"

"No, no it cannot!" She stumbled off toward the water. "Quickly, find something that floats!"

Sighing heavily, he followed her.

✝

Many hundreds, women and children included, had been crushed beneath the feet of the frantic, stampeding mob as they sought to flee the stadium through the narrow exit tunnels. Kuda and Semoon stepped gingerly amidst the grim scene. At one point, the Northman was forced to use his hands to pull apart a solid logjam of corpses that blocked their way. Repulsed by the sight of so many dead, terror-stricken faces, Semoon turned aside to gag and retch. Once beyond the gruesome barrier, they made their way out of the arena and into the deserted streets. It was unnaturally quiet. Nothing moved. Even the scattered bodies were free of flies and vermin. It seemed that all living things had fled the city, driven headlong by an all-consuming terror of the abomination that had invaded their world.

The two were finally able to cleanse their mired and blood-caked bodies at a public well that sat alongside one of the streets leading up to the palace. Each drank deeply, savoring the cool spring water from beneath the earth. The life-giving fluid trickled down their parched throats. After picking out some garments for Semoon from an overturned market stall, Kuda retrieved a longsword and javelin that had been abandoned in the street by their panicked owners. Few words passed between them as the pair trudged on toward the lofty palace, through streets that echoed with an eerie emptiness.

✝

An hour later they stood before the broad palace steps. Above them, the pall of dense smoke that hung over the city blocked out the sun. Several blazes had been ignited during the panicked rout and the smoke caused deep shadows to flicker and race across the white marble walls and golden towers. Kuda started up the wide stairs with Semoon close at his heels. Suddenly, she stopped. Motionless, she stood, staring at something. He turned to see what held her rapt attention. A bundle of rich clothing lay draped across the steps. It seemed to be quivering. Semoon's hand shook as she lifted aside the costly robes of imperial purple to reveal a desiccated old man, who was pulling himself slowly and painfully up the steps. The oldster turned his head toward her.

The Princess recoiled as though struck, her hand flying to her mouth. Kuda choked back an exclamation when he recognized the Emperor.

"Sister," the wizened ancient croaked. "Forgive me. None of it was my doing. I was ensorcelled by Shikrol's foul spells. I could not help myself. I was completely in his power, a slave to his dark ambition."

"I forgive you, brother," Semoon replied haltingly, her voice faint and breathless. "Shikrol is dead," she went on. "His magic destroyed. Let us help you now," she spoke kindly, extending her arms to raise him up.

"No! Do not touch me!" The quavering old voice pleaded."I carry an evil thing, you …"

Suddenly, the Emperor screamed, Kuda had never heard such a scream before. It seemed to be wrenched from deep inside the man's soul.

Face twisting in pain, he turned beseeching eyes upon them both. "Kill me," he cried out in a surprisingly strong voice. His whole body began trembling uncontrollably, as if he were freezing, despite the warm mugginess of the day. His shaking hands clutched at the steps.

Semoon staggered back into Kuda, who shoved her behind him.

"What is it?" she wailed helplessly. "What ails him?"

Kuda didn't respond. Grim faced, he stood glaring down at the writhing man, his sword raised. A bloody patch appeared on the Emperor's tunic, spreading rapidly across his lower chest. The fabric tore and split. There was a meaty squelch. Something punched outward in a spray of blood. Semoon let out a reverberating scream. Twisting and pulling, an insectoid head protruded out. Long feelers covered in crimson slime snaked out and stick-like legs flailed urgently to drag a flat body clear of dragging coils of entrails.

It flopped down onto the blood-splashed steps, leaving a huge ragged hole in the Emperor's chest. Before they could react, the creature skittered off up the staircase, swift as a startled rat.

Kuda dropped the sword and hefted the javelin. Drawing back his arm he took aim at the scampering creature and, with a heave of his huge shoulders, he launched the throwing spear. It arced up and swept down, pinning the disgusting insectile body to the marble. The thing screeched and writhed frantically before becoming still.

"What in the seven hells was that?" Kuda rasped, gazing fixedly at the Emperor's corpse.

"An incubus summoned by that black-hearted sorcerer," Semoon conjectured in a small defeated voice. "It must have been leeched onto my brother the whole time. Now it is clear how Shikrol bent the Emperor's will to his dark designs."

"A curse on all foul magickers," Kuda spat, drawing a deep, slow breath. "So, you are Queen now," he told her matter-of-factly.

For a moment, she stared back at him, her lovely face expressionless before she exclaimed, bitterly, "Queen of what?" She swept an arm out over the empty burning streets. "A city of the dead?"

"The living will return," Kuda stated with conviction. "Once they realize that big devil's turd will never be coming back. And the gods know, after what you've been through you've more than earned the right to the throne."

Recognizing the truth of his words, she straightened her shoulders and raised her chin. Angrily swiping at her tears with her palms, she asked, "How can I ever repay you?"

Kuda's eyes fell to the deep cleft of her breasts, which were heaving splendidly.

His teeth flashed in a lascivious grin. "Apart from the obvious, you mean?"

She found herself smiling back at him. "Yes, beside that."

"Well," his face hardened. "There is one thing."

✝

Dawn broke bright and golden over the great city of Bansaray. All morning, excited spectators had filed into The Heronium Stadium, packing the tiered seating to capacity. In the shade of the royal balcony, Queen Semoon sat upon the imperial throne, her posture regal and dignified as she gazed imperiously out over the amphitheater. All traces of the unholy pile of masonry had been removed, and the sands swept clean. At the center of that pristine circle of sand, under the glare of the bright sun, two men stood shoulder to shoulder, facing her. They were both warriors. Big fighting men, one sheathed from head to foot in close-fitting black mail, the other clad in a jerkin of good scale armor. Deep-toned trumpets sounded and the warriors bowed to the queen before turning to face each other.

"I thought you were the Queen's favorite barbarian, but it seems I was wrong." Skarasen spoke slowly as he drew a pair of short swords from their sheaths and backed slowly away to give himself fighting room. "She approached me with a contract for your death." The assassin watched the huge Northman steadily, his topaz-yellow gaze unwavering. "She even stipulated the time and place of your slaying."

Kuda slid the oiled blade of his heavy cavalry saber from its scabbard. "At my request," he rumbled, flinging the empty scabbard to one side. "When you see Yarrabay, tell him I sent you."

They met in a tempest of flashing steel.

TEARS OF THE GODS

ONE

On all sides, limitless as an ocean, the steppe stretched away from the man. Beneath him, his pony stumbled. He knew the animal well. Normally sure footed, it had reached the end of its endurance. It had been a long chase and it was time to end it, one way or another. Slumping forward in the saddle, he allowed the reins to drop from his hands. The pony walked on a little before stopping and hanging its head. The man waited a beat before slowly toppling from the saddle to the frozen ground, where he lay unmoving. An icy wind, cruel and unrelenting, stirred the furs upon his back. For a long time, nothing else moved.

With one ear pressed to the ground, he waited. Time expanded. The Universe contracted. But nothing happened.

Then, his numbed ear detected a vibration, the first cautious approach of his pursuers. They were wary, as they should be in this wild land. Three steppe-riders were approaching separately, from different directions. The hooves of their shaggy mounts slowly circling closer. He knew they would be holding their short, recurved bows at the ready, with arrows nocked. He also knew that they would be loath to put holes into the fine bearskin cloak that covered him. Silently, the riders stopped in unison.

The double creak of tightly drawn bowstrings made his flesh crawl. His muscles instinctively bunched in preparation to attack but, grinding his teeth, he fought down the urge. The stealthy slither of steel against leather told him that a man on foot had drawn a blade. Close. Good, now everything was simple.

With a demonic scream, he surged upward from the ground, both fists filled with steel. Ignoring the man on foot, he rushed headlong at the nearest rider. As the rider loosed his arrow, the pony shied and his shaft went wide.

The bearskin clad giant crashed into them with an impact that sent both rider and pony tumbling to the ground. With a crack like summer lightening, the beast's foreleg snapped. Screaming piteously, it writhed on the ground, trapping its rider beneath it. The giant rolled to his feet in time to meet the attack of the dismounted rider, who came leaping at him in a flurry of savage cuts. He countered the blows with a huge broadsword, its wide, dulled blade weaving an impenetrable shield. In their tribal dialect, the only mounted man shouted at his fellow warrior to step away from the big barbarian so he could get a clear shot. The warrior did not seem to hear and drove in with renewed fury. Cursing, the rider kicked at his pony, urging it into position for a shot. Desperately, the barbarian worked to keep his opponent between himself and the mounted bowman.

As they fought, the weather closed in. The horizons all around were now hidden behind drifting curtains of snow. The downed pony's screams ceased abruptly when the trapped rider drew his knife across its jugular. A jet of blood steamed high into the cold air. The momentary distraction allowed the barbarian to study his opponent. He was facing little more than a boy, barely out of his teens. The blows the boy delivered had strength and vigor, but lacked any skill or subtlety. Glancing up, he glimpsed the strained expression on the older rider's cursing face. Realization caused his lips to twitch into a grim smile; so, it was this old wolf's cub that now faced him. He flipped the hunting knife in his left hand, so that he now gripped the blade. Then, stepping inside the boy's next wild slash, he slammed the heavy hilt across the youth's face. Stunned, the young warrior staggered back. His Father's anguished cry echoed across the steppe as the big outlander dropped his sword and grabbed the boy, spinning him around to face his Father.

The older man lowered his bow at the sight of the hunting knife held across his son's throat. The boy struggled, but his youthful strength was no match for the outlander's iron hard thews. The Father barked a command and the young warrior's struggles ceased.

"Do you value your cub, old wolf?" The outlander spoke to the rider in the trade tongue, which was a common language for the steppes.

The older warrior raised his bow once again and took careful aim at his son's heaving chest. "He has shamed me."

As the barbarian felt his advantage sliding away, his mind raced furiously. "The fault is yours, old wolf. You thought me an easy kill, so you sent the boy on foot to whet his blade."

Once again, there came the creak of a taut bowstring.

"Your son has brought you no shame. He attacked without hesitation and fought bravely. You see how he fights me still."

He spoke on quickly. "Nobody has died here, yet. Nobody need die. I just need one pony in exchange for your son's life. One pony and you will see your grandchildren playing at your feet."

The Father's aim did not waver. The outlander felt the boy tense in expectation of the arrow's bite.

The snow fell heavier now, the wind carrying it across the undulating landscape in fitful bursts. In the dips and hollows, it gathered into drifts.

"Must we all die for an old man's pride?" Kuda finally asked.

Slowly, so very slowly, the sun's great red eye lowered itself toward the obscured horizon.

Slowly, so very slowly, the bow lowered, until the arrow pointed at the ground.

†

As he rode away through the driving snow, the hulking barbarian glanced back over his shoulder. The steppe-riders were working furiously to free their trapped comrade from under the dead pony. By the time they had done so, he would be long gone. It would be impossible, even for them, to track him through this blizzard. Also, he had pulled their teeth, three horse-bows hung from his saddle, part of the deal struck with the boy's father. He grinned, imagining the tongue lashing the boy would be receiving now. Still, the youth had survived, and the experience would serve him well. Lessons ... hard learned. Kuda's mind drifted back through his own hard learned lessons, back to his Northland home. He stared straight ahead, allowing the bittersweet memories to wash over him.

†

The stubby horse plodded on through the deepening drifts, its solitary progress accentuating the desolation of the surrounding plain. Upon its back, Kuda the barbarian sat perched in the bucket of a saddle, his thick-booted feet encased in box-like stirrups, his broadsword strapped across his back. The Northman's eyes flickered restlessly over the barren terrain, searching for anything that would give him some respite from the relentless wind; a cave or at least the lee of a rocky outcrop. Thick, dark clouds were bunching above him and the temperature was dropping further. He knew that, without shelter, he would not survive the night. An open campsite would find him frozen to death by morning. Shivering, he huddled deeper into his cocoon of thick furs.

A moment later, ahead of him in the gathering gloom of the snowflake-spotted dusk, a low shape interrupted the tedium of the steppe. In the grey light he discerned the welcome shape of a caravanserai. Impatiently, he dug both heels into the flanks of the sturdy pony beneath him.

†

As the pony swept into the hostel's walled courtyard, shadowy figures rose from where they squatted around glowing braziers. Kuda's mount slithered to a halt amidst a crowd of stocky, hard-eyed men. One of the men stepped up to Kuda's pony and pressed his hand to the beast's nostrils. The horse snorted in recognition and began nuzzling the man's palm. With an angry murmur, the crowd pressed forward, hands fumbling for weapons, fingers curling about hilts …

†

Esmira stared, wide-eyed, into the darkness, her shapely limbs trembling as, again and again, her mind returned to the horrific events of the past day. That morning, just as it had done for the past three weeks, the caravan she had been traveling with had struck camp and set out across the familiar ocean of waving winter grass. She recalled that, at that moment, she had never been so happy. She was on her way to the city of Khorrassa to become handmaiden to a high-born lady. Then the nightmare had begun. Disjointed images came back to her. The grassy plain had suddenly sprouted a mob of wild horsemen. With wolf-like cries, they swept down upon the travelers. The caravan guards formed up to protect the long straggling line of wagons and camels as best they could. But the horsemen galloped back and forth, bending the short, recurved bows they carried. Shaft after shaft whirred into the circle of her protectors; their arrow-riddled bodies falling beneath the raiders pounding hooves. She trembled as she remembered the leering, savage faces and the clutching hands on her soft flesh as she was dragged from the curtained wagon. A sob of loathing shook her voluptuous body.

"Don't cry, girl."

Esmira's heart leapt to fill her throat, choking off the sobs. She had thought herself alone in the caravanserai's capacious cellar. Calming herself, she narrowed her eyes to peer intently into the gloom. With a rustling of rich fabric, a figure materialized from the shadows. Sitting on the cold, earthen floor, she drew her knees up beneath her chin as she nervously regarded the stranger.

He was a middle-aged man wrapped in a voluminous quilted coat of fine wool. As he took a pace closer, she saw that his fashionable boots, bright yellow in color, had long, pointed upturned toes. His hair was clean and neatly combed. Likewise, a neatly combed beard covered his chin. Closer now, he stood looking down at her, a thin smile stretched across his face. She caught a whiff of his perfume as he lowered himself to the floor. They sat facing each other.

"The Kuruk will not harm you," he said in a soft voice.

For some reason, the man did not frighten her. Indeed, she felt reassured by his presence. She pulled her knees tighter into her body, clasped them with both arms and rested her chin on them. "Kuruk?" she asked.

"Our captors," he answered. "The name 'Kuruk' is nothing more than a grunt in their somewhat stilted tongue, but it translates as 'Lords of the Steppe.' A title they take very seriously indeed."

She looked curiously at him. "So you are a captive too?"

"Oh yes." The stranger's eye's twinkled. "Same time every year. I've become quite an expert on the Kuruk and their ways."

Esmira's brow furrowed. "I don't understand."

"Of course you don't, and you're frightened and confused and I'm only making it worse," he said, suddenly sounding concerned. "Allow me to introduce myself. My name is Hsuan Tsang. I am trade legate for the merchant's guild of the golden city of Khorrassa. At this time, every year, the guild begins dispatching trade goods westwards across the steppe. Every year, I join the first caravan of the trading season. And every year, the Kuruk waylay the caravan and take me prisoner."

The girl tensed, her generous mouth opening in surprise.

Tsang raised a placating hand before continuing.

"Furthermore, every year, I am released and allowed to return safely back to Khorrassa."

Before she could interrupt him, the legate took a deep breath and launched into an explanation. "The Kuruk are a race of proud warriors. For generations, they have swept across the steppes, pillaging, looting and generally causing mayhem, which was all very well." He held up an admonishing finger. "When the Kuruk were nothing more than a few roving tribes. But nowadays, they are a single nation under their Great Khan, and their numbers are limitless. They thrive to the detriment of any other peoples they encounter, people they either absorb or destroy." He spread his hand in a helpless gesture. "They are turning great swathes of this continent into a wasteland."

Esmira blinked at the dim form that sat only a few feet from her. Her eyes were growing heavy. She was bone-tired and felt weary, but she fought her overwhelming exhaustion as the merchant went on with his speech.

"So, the guild need to maintain functioning caravan routes, and the Kuruk, despite themselves, must allow major trade routes to stay open if the steppes are not to become completely uninhabitable. What is required then is a compromise."

Tsang paused, a grave look on his face. "Compromise is not an easy concept for the Kuruk to grasp. Their culture, built as it is, is founded upon a thousand years of mindless violence. They are a tribal people, smug in their own assumed superiority. Yet there has been some progress, hence the annual ritual of my kidnapping and ransom. You see, the guild I represent are, in fact, paying a yearly toll to the steppe-riders for the full use of the ancient caravan routes, paying it in such a way that it does not offend the Kuruks' towering arrogance."

"Ransom!" Esmira blurted out. "Perhaps my employers will pay a ransom for me."

Tsang's face took on a pained expression. "I'm afraid it's not as simple as that. My so-called ransom is the result of several years of delicate negotiations. Negotiations that have cost the lives of dozens of trade legates. They …"

She cut him off, her voice strident. "But you said the Kuruk would not harm me."

He made calming motions with his hands. "I believe that to be so, but if you could just answer one question for me?" he asked soothingly.

"Very well," she agreed in a brittle voice.

"Did, erm, did …" the merchant began uneasily. "Did your abductors molest you at all?"

"Of course, they did. They laid their filthy hands upon my person," she answered hotly, her pretty face a mask of indignation.

"Quite, quite." His voice dropped to nothing more than a strained whisper. "But did they, er, invade your very private place?"

"What!" The girl shrieked, incredulous. "I would be lying dead upon the frozen ground with the guards had they dared. I would have taken my own life before one of those pigs …"

"I see, I see." Tsang fluttered his hands wildly, stilling the girl's outburst.

The silence that followed stretched taut between them until Tsang gave a delicate cough.

Esmira tilted her chin toward him. "What made you ask such a thing?"

The flamboyantly attired man's answer came floating out of the shadows. "The fact that the Kuruk left you intact confirms their intentions toward you. They mean to sell you as a slave.Beautiful young girls fetch a good price at the auctions, but virgins are particularly prized."

The words were spoken patiently and gently but each one struck Esmira with the force of a hammer blow. She couldn't speak or move. She could only sit, immobile, letting the horror of it bubble up inside her. A scream forced its way up her throat, but as she opened her mouth to give vent, a great crash reverberated through the underground room.

✝

The cellar's thick, wooden door smashed back on its hinges. Torchlight streamed into the cold earthen chamber. A massive figure hurtled headfirst through the doorway to bounce heavily down the cellar's stone steps. At the top of the steps, several steppe-riders crowded shoulder to shoulder in the doorframe, their malicious eyes glaring at the man who lay sprawled at the foot of the stairway. One of them threw a blazing torch that flared like a comet before bouncing off the prone man's head in a shower of sparks. Grinning, they withdrew, tugging the door shut behind them.

Silence returned, broken only by the fitful spluttering of the burning torch. Without a word, Tsang slowly eased himself to his feet. Esmira rose with him, stretching her long shapely legs to ease the stiffness in them. She stuck close to the merchant as he retrieved the spluttering torch. Side by side, they warily advanced upon the sprawled body. As they drew closer with the torch held high, the concealing shadows fled. Esmira found herself gazing down at the strangest looking person she had ever laid eyes upon.

A giant of a man, clad only in a loincloth, whose skin was weathered to a coppery sheen.

"Is he dead?" she whispered.

Tsang didn't answer, instead he bent low over the body, his slender fingers absently stroking the neatly trimmed goatee that sprouted from his chin. The merchant saw that the prone man's long, black coarse hair was braided in places, and thickly matted with blood.

"He lives," Tsang announced finally, dropping his voice to almost a whisper. "But he will not awaken this night. He has taken quite a beating, it appears. It is a great wonder that he breathes at all."

"I have never seen his like before," the girl admitted, still whispering despite Tsang's diagnosis.

"I do not doubt it. Even for someone as well traveled as I, the sight of a clansman from one of the Great Northern tribes is rare."

She took a quick step back, her hand flying to her mouth. "I thought the tales of Northern giants were nothing more than children's fables."

"Indeed, they are." Tsang spoke in reassuring tones, attempting to soothe the girl, who seemed on the verge of panic. "The Northern peoples are flesh and blood, as we are. Although, they generally grow to a more prodigious size and strength than we Southern peoples. I must admit, though," he went on, turning to study the unconscious Northerner once more, "that this specimen would probably seem like a giant even among his own, huge brethren."

TEARS OF THE GODS

Somewhat reassured, Esmira edged closer. "What are those?" she asked, pointing an unsteady finger at some markings on the giant's arms.

Tsang peered down at the white scars of old wounds that patterned the tanned skin. "The marks of blades. He is undoubtedly a warrior."

"He is a brute," she hissed. "A brute from the edge of the world."

"That too," Tsang agreed, nodding.

One arm, bulging with muscle, pushed against the floor as the Northman lurched onto his side. Through a mask of blood, two glittering eyes stared up at them. Esmira screamed and fled. Tsang stood rooted to the spot, mouth gaping as, slowly and with infinite care, the gore-smeared Northerner heaved himself to his feet. Monstrous and alien in the flickering light, the barbarian swept the underground chamber with a befuddled gaze. Tsang's mouth began working but for once, he seemed lost for words. The big man ignored him, his eyes coming to rest upon the cowering girl.

Under his scrutiny, Esmira backed away until she felt the rough wood of a stack of beer kegs digging into her spine. She could retreat no further. In one swift movement, she stooped and plucked a slim dagger from a hidden sheath stitched inside one of her soft felt boots. A brief glance down at the blade in her hand reminded her of the day her father had presented her with the weapon. The time he had deeply urged her to take her own life, rather than bring shame upon the family. A steely resolve swelled within her as she remembered the oath she had sworn to him that day.

The barbarian shook his bloody head, as though clearing it of cobwebs, before shoving the gaping merchant to one side. Tsang staggered and fell, the torch spinning from his hand. Ignoring the sprawled man, the Northerner began walking unsteadily across the cellar toward the girl.

Stifling a scream, Esmira fought to remain calm as she positioned the dagger's point just below her left breast. Curling her fingers tightly around the hilt, she closed her eyes and muttered a small prayer, asking her Gods to receive her. When she opened her eyes again, the barbarian was looming over her, his dark bulk filling her vision. Nausea overwhelmed her as an unwashed stink clogged her delicate nostrils. He stretched out a huge hand toward her. She shifted her weight and felt the dagger's needle point slide into her flesh. The scarred hand reached over her and grabbed a beer keg. Pulling on it, he managed to drag the small barrel from the stack behind her. Turning on his heel the barbarian strode off with the cask tucked under one brawny arm. Esmira's vision blurred. The dagger fell from her fingers as she flopped to the floor of hard-packed dirt.

Tsang sat up just in time to see the girl collapse in a dead faint. On the other side of the cellar, there was a splintering crash. Turning his head, he saw the barbarian gulping ale from a stoved in cask. The merchant sighed, it was going to be a long night.

TWO

Brittle snow crunched beneath Kuda's bare feet. A pony thundered past his left shoulder, spraying him with stinging chips of ice. His hands were bound together in front of him with rawhide strips. A rope was looped around his neck, its other end tied to the back of a rattling, two-wheeled wagon, drawn by a single lumbering ox. The steaming beast moved at a steady pace, tugging Kuda and the wagon along behind it.

Kuda's head throbbed. The last thing he could clearly recall was being dragged from his mount by an angry mob after riding through the caravanserai's gates. His hangover was a mystery to him. Glancing around, he could see steppe-riders to eitherside, and others ranging ahead. Their horses moved with long, rapid strides, covering the ground with a smooth, measured beat while their riders sat at ease in their deep, comfortable saddles. He was completely naked but for a brief loincloth that twisted about his loins. The cold ate into him. With his breath pluming before his eyes, he quickened his pace in an attempt to keep warm.

Without warning, a vicious pain exploded between his shoulder blades, driving him to his knees. Kuda twisted around to see a horseman almost on top of him. The rider glared down at the outlander, his eyes like saber-points. In one hand, he carried a whip of oiled leather. Its sinuous length curled down to fleck the snow with crimson. Kuda could feel blood trickling down his back. The rope about his neck snapped taut, pulling him to his feet. The whip parted the frozen air with a loud crack as it came again to slice across his shoulder, winding its way around his naked torso. Kuda did not flinch or cry out at the burning pain and the rider spurred his pony past him, half-turning in the saddle to fix him with a look of utter hatred. It was the young man he had shamed in the presence of his Father.

†

For the rest of the day Kuda trudged along behind the wagon, his world reduced to a set of wheel tracks in the snow and the deep grunting breaths of the ox as it plodded forward. The tribesmen remained in their saddles and ate from packages of smoke-cured meat and dry milk curds. Kuda was offered neither food nor rest and, as the day wore on, his mood turned savage. The young man frequently returned to lash at him. By the time the sun began dipping toward the flat horizon, Kuda's back was a lattice of raised welts and bleeding cuts.

†

It was growing dark when he felt eyes upon him. Lifting his head, he saw a woman's face peering out at him through a gap in the thick hide curtains that hung across the rear of the covered wagon. His gaze sharpened; not a woman, a very beautiful girl who seemed vaguely familiar. Her soft brown eyes regarded him for a moment before the heavy curtains fell back into place. He struggled to recall where he had seen her before, but his brain, numbed with cold and fatigue, refused to co-operate. The curtains twitched again and a dark bundle dropped to the snow. He staggered forward to snatch at the parcel with stiff, clumsy fingers. He unfurled a thick fur cloak and with difficulty, draped it around his shoulders. The relief from the knife-edged wind was immediate and blissful. Ignoring the stinging pain from his back, he pulled the luxurious fur up around his ears.

†

TEARS OF THE GODS

Uracc looked about him and felt despair engulf his soul. He could see warriors from five separate tribes riding together, as though they were brothers of the same blood. They were not his brothers. His brothers would have left the mongrel outlander's remains upon the freezing steppe. That oaf had caused him to lose face, and vengeance was called for. His true brothers would have ensured that vengeance, but these tribesmen didn't share his vindictiveness for they were not of his tribe: the Claw tribe. They kept the outlander alive in the hopes of making a profit off him when they reached the slave-pits. Uracc spat. Since when did the Kuruk concern themselves with trade? No sooner had the warring tribes been gathered together under the Great Khan's banner, they started behaving like fat-arsed city merchants. It was a point of great pride to Uracc that his tribe had been the last to kneel before the Great Khan, the last to erect their yurts about the Ziggurat. The Ziggurat. The young warrior made a discreet sign to ward off evil as his thoughts turned unbidden to that ancient brooding structure and its equally forbidding occupant. Why had the Khan chosen such an evil and unholy place to assemble the host? He shivered inside his lacquered breastplate. Such questions were best left to the shamans. He had brooded long enough. Taking up his bloodstained whip, he urged his pony into a canter.

✝

Stumbling along in a half-daze, his flayed back throbbing with rhythmic pain beneath the fur mantle, Kuda could feel warmth and life returning to his frozen limbs. His thoughts turned to the young woman in the wagon, whose act of kindness had probably saved his life. A vision of her beautiful face came to him and he hoped he might get the chance to repay her properly. Grinning widely at the notion, he plodded on. Two steps later, the grin, barely formed, twisted into a grimace of agony as the fur was brutally wrenched away, taking with it long strips of his mangled flesh. A heavy blow sent him reeling to the ground.

He lay unmoving while the whip struck at him like an angry viper. He felt nothing. All sensation had been crowded out by a great, heated pressure that was building within his chest, as though a furnace door had been suddenly flung open there. There was a roaring in his ears and a red mist descended before his eyes. Kuda the outlander, the victim, was no more. In his place lay a savage, primeval beast, honed to destruction and merciless beyond words. A feral snarl ripped from deep within its throat as the beast leapt to its feet, snapping the rope that secured it. With every taut sinew and muscle on its hulking frame quivering with the lust to kill, it turned toward its tormentor.

Uracc's pony, bred to the wild, saw the red-eyed beast loping toward it and shied away in terror. The arrogant young rider saw nothing but a captive asking to be slaughtered. He tugged at the reins, trying to turn the horse's head, but he was too late. With a primordial roar, the beast lunged at the pony's flank, wedging its massive shoulders under the petrified creature's belly. With a mighty bone-creaking surge of effort, it lifted both pony and rider into the air. For a moment, the tableau froze. Then the panicked steed began kicking its legs, whinnying in terror. The beast's shoulders heaved with one final explosive surge before its burden flew sideways to hit the ground with a great thud.

†

"What's happening now?" Esmira asked, her voice low and urgent.

Tsang pressed his face up against the gap in the curtains. "The Northman has collapsed and the riders are closing in. The young tribesman is trying to rise but he seems to be pinned beneath his pony, which has a broken neck by the look of it."

"Is the barbarian dead?"

"I cannot say. Probably. I would not be surprised if his heart hasn't simply burst. The strain put upon it by such an exertion must have been phenomenal."

"He's dead then," the girl stated flatly.

"The riders are kicking him. Wait! Yes, he stirs. He lives still!" Tsang's voice strained with disbelief.

"It's your fault," the girl accused petulantly. "You should have let him freeze to death. Why did you have to give him that cloak?"

The merchant turned his head toward the reclining maiden, a thoughtful expression on his face. He stared at her silently for a long moment before speaking. "I am no longer a young man and, within a handful of years, I will be an old one," he sighed. "When death comes, I'll accept it. I'll lay down and die because that is what is expected of me. I accept that, for all men, there is a time to die. Yet," he held up one slender finger, "as I watched the Northman today, I glimpsed something irreconcilable with that iron law. I witnessed not just a struggle against death, but a man renouncing the very idea of death. You see," he went on, stroking his thin mustaches and warming to his theme, "a civilized man in the same hopeless predicament, with a head full of preconceived horrors and visions of agonizing ends, would simply curl up and die. Not this barbarian, not this unwashed lout who would be turned away from the city gates." His words began tumbling over each other as he drew himself up to square his thin shoulders. "Unburdened, his spirit soars free, spurning all doubts, defying both men and Gods! Don't you see?" He leaned toward her, his voice becoming low and earnest. "He is the essence of all we have lost since we retreated into our civilized shells. A being of true nobility."

The girl stared unbelievingly at the older man. Her mind reeling. How could this rich and powerful city merchant actually admire the horrid savage that lay half-dead in the snow outside? Or was it something else? Her fine brow creased in thought. Perhaps the outlander's display of strength had enlightened Tsang in a different way. The light that now shone in the trader's eyes could have more to do with profit than philosophy. After all, such brute power must be worth a great deal in some quarters. Esmira arched one cynical eyebrow. The barbarian had certainly touched the old man's soul, all the way down to his purse.

✝

Several fur-capped warriors took hold of Uracc's dead pony and tried to shift it. The lifeless beast refused to budge. Shaking their heads in disbelief, the men stood back. Turning aside, they began pacing out the exact distance of the throw. Voices were raised in argument. Eventually, a figure was agreed upon and, once again, the warriors stood around with their fingers hooked in their sword belts, shaking their heads in disbelief.

Then someone remembered Uracc who still lay fuming and cursing, with one leg trapped beneath his dead mount. Brod, the nominal leader of the raiding party, walked over to where the felled warrior lay. He moved with a slightly rolling gait, his bowed legs the result of years spent on horseback. "Do you know how far you have been flung?" he asked the trapped man in a serious tone.

Uracc swore and beat impotently at the dead pony.

"Fifteen cubits," Brod intoned gravely, ignoring Uracc's outburst. Without another word, he turned away and began pacing out the distance again. He stopped when he reached Kuda's sprawled and motionless body. "Don't move him," he ordered the gathered steppe-riders. "Build a fire here and spread a poultice on his back, then wrap him in furs. You two," he barked at a pair of mounted warriors, "pass your ropes about the dead pony and drag it away before the carcass upsets all our mounts."

Uracc staggered to his feet the second the horse was pulled off him. Immediately he began tugging at his sword but it was too hopelessly bent out of shape to leave its scabbard.

Giving up, he instead drew a short, broad-bladed dagger from a sheath at the small of his back and with a blood-curdling scream threw himself toward the helpless barbarian.

Brod bellowed a command and Uracc was instantly lost to sight beneath a scrum of wrestling warriors.

✝

The sun rose stealthily behind a thick grey rampart of cloud, its wan light doing little to dispel the long hours of darkness. Men stirred while above them dawn flights of duck beat their way westwards. When the curtains of thick hide at the rear of the wagon were abruptly hauled apart, Esmira merely opened one eye and huddled deeper into her furs. Brod stood holding the flaps open allowing gusts of chill air to scour the interior of the wagon that had been snug beneath its canopy of stretched canvas. Tsang sat up and peered about him just in time to see Brod turn and jerk a thumb toward the wagon bed. A bulky inert form was manhandled over the wagon's tailboard. Kuda landed in a heap upon the expensive furs.

Esmira sat bolt upright, her eyes flashing. "You needn't think I'm traveling with that stinking animal in here! He's probably infested, the furs will be crawling within the hour."

She pointed a trembling finger at Brod. "Remove him. Do you hear me? Remove him."

Brod showed his strong white teeth in a broad grin. Although he couldn't understand the maiden's words, her meaning was clear enough. He responded in the trade-tongue common to all peoples. "Come and ride with me then, girl. We can keep each other warm. I'll wrap you in my arms and whisper love poems in your ear all the way to the Ziggurat."

The warriors, who had formed a tight circle around the rear of the wagon laughed uproariously as Esmira paled and sank wordlessly back into her furs.

Brod turned to Tsang, his face serious once again. "Don't let the outlander die, merchant. You of all people should appreciate good merchandise when you see it." With that, he was gone and the curtains flopped back into place.

†

The sun had cleared the horizon by no more than a hand's breadth when the oxen strained against their harnesses and the line of captured wagons rippled into motion. Unconscious, Kuda lay motionless on his stomach in the bed of the two-wheeled cart as it jounced and rolled over the steppe. Tsang tended to the barbarian's wounds, frowning over the flayed back as he anointed the torn flesh with a salve.

Esmira looked on, her beautiful face twisted into a scowl. "Why bother?" she snapped. "He's probably going to die and even if he lives to mount the slave block, you'll see no profit from it."

Tsang shrugged. "I am a merchant, and that warrior was correct in his assessment. This Northman is a valuable piece of merchandise, the like of which is rarely seen in these lands. He would make a formidable arena fighter or a rich man's bodyguard. Once he's on his feet, he should fetch a good price."

The girl snorted but said nothing more. With difficulty, Tsang managed to wrap the barbarian's upper body in tight bandages of clean linen. Breathing heavily, the trader turned to Esmira. "Help me turn him onto his back," he wheezed.

She looked shocked. "He stinks!" she protested.

"He'll stink more if he dies," Tsang pointed out reasonably.

Grumbling under her breath the maiden moved forward and took hold of one brawny shoulder. Working together, they managed to turn the Northman.

"There." She sat back, wiping her hands down her furs.

Tsang nodded toward a bowl of water that was close by her. "Place a damp cloth across his forehead before you sit down again."

Tutting loudly, she wet a cloth. Stooping over the big outlander, she arranged the cloth, ready to place it on his brow and lowered her eyes. The face beneath her was a hard face, a man's face, a warrior's face. A look of disdain distorted her comely features. What could a creature such as this ever offer her? Himself? What a catch. Two hundred and fifty pounds of muscle, bones and scars supporting a face like a granite cliff. As the cold cloth touched the barbarian's skin, his eyes flickered open. She gave a small gasp of surprise. His extraordinary bright green eyes fixed on her for a moment before closing once again. In a flash, she retreated to the wagon's furthest corner and began dragging heavy furs up to her chin.

✝

As evening approached, the wagons creaked to a halt. Tsang and Esmira sat up with sudden interest. All around them, guttural voices began calling to each other and hoof beats began pounding up and down the line of stationary carts. Heaving themselves from their furs, the pair scrambled up to peer through a gap in the canopy.

The wagons had stopped on the crest of a rise and they found themselves looking down into the basin of land beyond.

Wreathed in the blue smoke of camp fires and shaded by the deepening dusk, a mass of men, animals and tents filled the vast crater before them. The tents were round, low huts called yurts, a latticework of wood covered with stretched skins and felt. The yurts were not permanent structures. They were designed to be dismantled and carried on carts; the Kuruk were a nomadic people. Their eyes passed quickly over the encampment, drawn to the extraordinary structure that loomed at the center of the depression. A squat, stone pyramid soared a hundred feet into the air. A flight of steps led up the face of the pyramid to the portico of a strange looking temple that crowned its summit.

At a yelled command, the carts started down the beaten-earth road that led into the huge camp. First they passed vast pens of livestock, mostly horses, sheep and oxen, before entering the busy streets of churned mud that threaded through the city of yurts. Lamps and mutton-fat torches flared at every intersection. In their yellow light, Tsang recognized warriors from several different tribes rubbing shoulders with each other. As always, he marveled at how the Great Khan had managed to bring them all together when only a single generation ago they had been nothing but a bunch of squabbling, blood-thirsty horse tribes.

The line of carts lurched to a halt at the edge of a large open space, which, Tsang surmised, would become a marketplace during the day. He knew that merchants had been drawn from every land to this vast gathering of nomads and their fat purses. Upon arrival, every trader paid the Khan's clerks a tax to set up their ramshackle stalls. Tsang spared little thought for such insignificant peddlers. The tribute, or ransom, as the Kuruk preferred to call it, that he was here to negotiate, would amount to a sum far beyond their reckoning. A King's ransom would be paid by the rich cities of the steppe to keep their lifelines, the caravan routes, open for another trading season. Tsang's reverie was broken when the curtains were whipped back and a tribesman thrust his flat-featured face into the wagon. "Out!" he barked impatiently.

THREE

Kuda sat staring moodily out through the heavy metal grille that blocked the entrance of the cave. It was not really a cave, but an overhang where the soft, red sandstone had been dug out of the crater's side to form an enclosure. There was a stone hearth against the back wall of the shelter, and the low roof was soot-stained. Littering the floor were the bones of sheep and small mammals, remnants of meals that had been prepared at the hearth. He was not alone. Other men moved about the shallow cave, grimacing and scratching, sleeping and eating. Despite them all being captives of the Kuruk, none of them wore chains, and they were all fed and treated well. All were condemned to lifelong slavery, waiting to be sold at the forthcoming auctions. Beyond the grille, there was constant movement with warriors and slaves coming and going from the horse lines, and men drifting toward the toilet pits on personal business. The air was blue and thick with the smoke of hundreds of cooking fires. Women moved throughout the camp bearing steaming rice pots and doling out the midday meal. Few sentries were set and little order enforced, it seemed.

Watching the women took Kuda's mind back to the girl who had saved his life. He recalled her leaning close over him as she tended to his injuries. Her skin was flawless and smooth, and a tangle of dark ringlets framed her pretty face. He was in her debt and he longed to see her again. He resolved to find out where the female captives were being held as soon as he could.

A short, wiry man with a weather-beaten look flopped down next to the huge, brooding barbarian. Kuda barely spared the newcomer a glance. His name was Stul and for some reason the sinewy hillman had decided to make the outlander his best friend. He was holding two platters of hot mutton, one of which he passed to Kuda. Kuda accepted the food and the two men sat quietly, eating while watching the snow fall thickly beyond the locked grille. Kuda relished the silence for he knew it would not last. Stul liked to talk and never tired of the sound of his own voice.

Throwing the empty platter down, the smaller man belched explosively. "Not bad eh, Kuda? Not bad at all," he exclaimed, using the common trade tongue while wiping his hands down clothes that were already shiny with grease.

Kuda ignored him, but the shorter man rattled on without waiting for a response. "Of course, they're just fattening us up for the slave block so we fetch a better price. Nobody pays good money for a sickly slave."

Between endless repetitions of the obvious, Kuda had learned from Stul's endless talk over the last few weeks that he was of the Blue Mountain tribe. It was the only tribe that, Stul maintained, had not bowed their knee to the Great Khan. His tribe's continued resistance was a source of great pride to Stul, who bragged about his brothers in arms and their mountain stronghold, where they still held out against the Khan's troops. The wiry man puffed out his chest when he spoke of the raids he and his blood brothers regularly carried out against the Khan's forces and how they rode circles around the lowlanders who had been sent to hunt them down.

"How did you come to be captured then?" Kuda asked with mock innocence, interrupting the braggart's flow.

Stul's grimy, pox-scarred face twisted in disgust. "Ill luck!" he spat. "I lingered too long in a herdsman's tent. Those dung-eating lowlanders caught me unawares."

Kuda's eyes flickered sideways toward the smaller man. "Was she worth it?"

The tribesman's tilted eyes took on a faraway glaze. "She was more beautiful than any woman I had ever seen," he whispered reverentially. "A flower of a girl, with thick glossy dark hair and eyes that could drown a man. She ..." He broke off suddenly, eyes tightening in bitter anger. "... Her father. That sheep-raping herder, had no respect for our passion and told the Kuruk where to find us."

Kuda laughed, clapping the mountain man on the back. "There is always a woman to tempt us into folly," he guffawed.

Stul shrugged and laughed also.

"Now, tell me," Kuda stilled the laughter with a question, "has anyone ever escaped these Kuruk?"

Stul snorted dismissively. "Where would you escape to? The steppe stretches to the ends of the earth in every direction. The Kuruk would thank you for trying to escape as you would be providing them with sport. They would probably grant you a head start to make the chase more interesting for them. Anyway," he shook his head slowly, "only a madman would risk the open steppe in winter. You blundered into their world easily enough, Northman, but leaving it again is another matter. Better to take your chances on the slave block."

Kuda's glower went unnoticed by the little man, who was still blathering.

"Professional slave traders come here for the auctions," he went on. "They know the Kuruk take many captives during their far-ranging raids. If you're lucky, one will buy you and take you back to a soft rich city where they will sell you on again at a greater price. That is your only means of escape from this hole."

Kuda took a deep breath in an effort to control the sudden wave of anger that rose in his breast. The thought of meekly surrendering to a life of slavery was maddening. Biting down on his fury, he asked another question. "Why do these whoresons gather here anyway? Out in the middle of nowhere in winter. Why don't they capture a prosperous city to dwell in during the winter months?"

"The Ziggurat," Stul answered in an almost reverent hush.

"That ancient pile of stone? What about it?"

Stul's eyes slid away from the barbarian. "I cannot speak of it."

Kuda's eyes widened in amazement. "By the seven hells, I never thought I'd stumble upon something that would shut you up."

The small man shifted uneasily. "You're right, it is ancient. No-one can remember who built it or why, or even if it was built by human hand. It is even rumored to have just appeared overnight. For as long as anyone can remember, the steppe-riders have shunned this place."

"Why?" Kuda prompted, eyeing the dark-haired stump of a clansman, who looked as if he was on the verge of a self-induced panic.

Stul swallowed hard. "A dragon resides within those walls."

Kuda's face flickered with annoyance. "Dragon, pah!" He spat out a curse. "I have heard tales of dragons in every land I have ever passed through. Yet, I have never met anyone who has ever seen one."

"This one is real," Stul said hurriedly. "All have seen its fiery breath. You will too if you stay here long enough."

"Where?" Kuda snapped. "Where will I see it?"

"Out on the steppe. There are tunnels that are said to lead beneath the Ziggurat. That is where the dragon sleeps, and when he wakes, the ground trembles and he breathes great flames from the tunnel mouths."

The barbarian blew out an exasperated breath. "You make no sense. Why would the Kuruk gather here then? If what you say is true, a fire breathing dragon gives them even more reason not to linger hereabouts."

"The dragon has a keeper. It is neither man, woman nor beast. Though, the Great Khan communes with it. He enters the Ziggurat alone."

"Why would he do such a thing?"

"It is said that the Khan wishes to harness the dragon to his armies. With such a beast at the head of his horde, he could conquer the world. The cities of man would throw open their gates at his approach."

Kuda shook his head slowly. "And why would a being, who has a dragon for a pet, listen to a jumped-up, flea-bitten nomad from the steppes, even if he does call himself Great Khan?"

"The tears of the Gods. That's why." Stul's voice sank to a whisper. "The keeper desires them. When they fall from the sky the Khan sends his riders to search them out and bring them back to the Ziggurat."

The giant Northerner clenched his fists. "Do you take me for a fool, you goat-herding little shit?" he rasped harshly, his face hardening. "Squatting beside me, spouting nonsense for your own amusement, at my expense."

Stul's face paled. "I cannot say any more. It is ill luck to speak of such things," he spluttered and, jumping to his feet, scrambled quickly away.

†

One morning, the locked door set into the holding pen's grille swung open and the captives were led out into the wintry sunshine. Their overseer, Nazim, an olive-skinned paunchy individual, quickly herded together and shepherded the captives through the muddy streets of domed yurts. Unfettered and unguarded, they shambled along. They passed by lounging groups of steppe-riders, whose squat faces remained as blank as carvings as they followed the grouped slaves with their eyes. Bored beyond reason by a long winter of inactivity, the warriors fingered their hilts and prayed that one of the slaves would attempt to escape. None did.

Before long, the gloomy procession entered an open-air slave-market where wooden stakes had been hammered into the ground. Without delay, each slave was shackled to a stake and stripped of their clothes. Left to stand in only a brief loincloth, Kuda hunched his shoulders against the cold. A brisk wind blew across the cleared ground but it had little bite to it and he could detect spring in the passing air. He glanced around, his eyes coming to rest on another set of embedded poles on the far side of the cleared area, to which women had been shackled. He scanned the rows of females until his searching eyes came to rest on a group of younger, attractive girls. The girls had not been stripped naked as the men had. Indeed, care had been taken with their dress and cosmetics to accentuate their comeliness. Kuda recognized her immediately. The girl from the wagon was clad in a red gown that was as filmy and light as woodsmoke.

†

Esmira saw the great oaf of a barbarian staring at her and shivered, not just from the cold. He was standing there, stark naked, his superbly muscled frame straight and proud, not looking the least bit ashamed. His eyes were openly devouring her in such a way that left little doubt as to his intentions toward her. She turned away from him, transferring her gaze to a group of men who had just entered the market place. Their robes and furs looked expensive. From the way the overseers bowed and groveled before them, she surmised that they were prosperous merchants who had come early to view the slaves on offer.

With a swish of silken robes, the party approached the women. Esmira quickly decided that a rich master's protection was exactly what she needed just now. Swallowing her pride, she allowed a lazy, languorous smile to part her full red lips. Fixing the men with a sultry gaze, she threw back the shawl from her shoulders and shook out her raven hair so that it flew out like a banner on the wind.

†

The auction block was merely a pile of raised dirt with a short ramp leading up to it. Nazim was acting as auctioneer. To his side sat a clerk, behind a folding table piled high with parchments that would become bills of sale. The crowd of bidders and spectators were in a festive mood and cheered Nazim as he mounted the platform and raised his hands for silence.

Waiting until the good-natured jeers and catcalls subsided, he began to speak. "By order of the Great Khan, I am authorized to offer for sale, to the highest bidder, a superior selection of slaves taken from lands far and wide." He broke off and signed to his burly assistants to start the proceedings.

One by one, the slaves were pushed up onto the platform and presented to the crowd, while Nazim raised his voice to extol their virtues. The crowd seemed uninterested in the first few groups of slaves, who stood there with stooped shoulders and vacant expressions. Nazim began sweating heavily as he tried to rouse the crowd's interest in such apathetic specimens. Eventually, there was some desultory bidding, but most of the slaves remained unsold and were led back to the slave-pens.

It seemed that the crowd, especially the moneyed traders, were biding their time. They knew well enough that the finest merchandise was always presented last. An hour dragged by before Stul was pushed onto the block. He stood there, a sour-faced, bitter-eyed creature with matted filthy hair. Sighing heavily, Nazim managed to come up with a short list of the tribesman's supposed positive attributes. No one was fooled, however, and the crowd jeered and made rude noises. The mountain man was an obvious troublemaker, one who would run at the first opportunity. In any event, the people of the Blue Mountain tribe were not noted for their work ethic. The slave-master scanned the crowd in vain for someone to start the bidding, but none were foolhardy enough. And so, to the sound of an ironic cheer, Stul was taken back to the pens and an uncertain future.

Kuda was next to be led up to the block. He stood tall and straight staring over the heads of the crowd. A magnificent specimen with every muscle standing proud beneath the tanned and weathered skin of his chest and arms. At the sight of him, an excited buzz of chatter rose from the mob. There was a covered stand along one side of the market, with three rows of benches raised high enough for the wealthiest buyers to watch the proceedings in some degree of comfort. The stir of interest caused by Kuda's arrival on the block caused the benches there to creak under the shifting weight of their occupants.

Sensing profit, Nazim grinned hugely. "This lot is the slave, Kuda. He is about thirty years of age and is believed to be a clansman of some Northern tribe. A rarity indeed!" In his enthusiasm, Nazim took a step toward the huge man and reached out a hand to squeeze a bulging bicep. With murder in his eyes Kuda's head whipped around and the slave-master jumped back. A huge cheer broke out at this. The auctioneer had to wait for it to subside before he went on. "As you can see, he is a fierce warrior and would make a formidable bodyguard. He can ride, is skilled with weapons and speaks the trade tongue well enough. He would undoubtedly also give good service as a caravan guard."

"Five hundred deniers!" shouted one of the rich traders.

"And one hundred," barked out another.

Nazim clapped his hands together and eagerly acknowledged the bids while Kuda swept his gaze along the rows of expensively attired traders. His eyes fell upon one who looked vaguely familiar. The bidding went quickly to fifteen hundred deniers. The competitors were a caravan master and the merchant Kuda thought he recognized.

"Two thousand," sang out the merchant.

The caravan master made a disgusted face and waved a hand dismissively.

Nazim cried out exultantly, "Sold to that noble merchant of Khorrassa, Hsuan Tsang!"

†

Uracc sat his mount at the edge of the crowd. From under hooded lids, his cold eyes fixed upon the barbarian. So, he pondered, the merchant from Khorrassa had bought the outlander. That meant that the barbarian would be leaving the camp with the trader once 'ransom' negotiations had been completed. He grinned wolfishly. The Khan's law forbade revenge killings within the encampment but out on the open steppe, they would be at his mercy.

†

Nazim raised his arms to still the mob. "Peace now, good people. I know what you have been waiting for," he laughed, winking at the men in the crowd. "The time has come to reward your patience." He gestured and there was a masculine hum of approval as the first beautiful young woman sashayed up onto the block. Nazim heaved a sigh of relief. His job was easy now, the bidding would go quickly.

Esmira ascended the slave block to stand blinking at the raucous crowd.

"Stand proudly," Nazim hissed at her before addressing the crowd. "I now present to you a jewel beyond price. This beautiful maiden has been examined by the Great Khan's own physician, and he has given his assurance that she has never known a man." A mutter of appreciation rose from the audience. "Walk," the slave-master ordered her. Hesitantly at first, but then with more assurance Esmira made a slow circle of the platform. "Note the fluidity and grace of her movements," said the auctioneer. "Note the sweetness of her figure, the straightness of her back and the proud carriage of her head."

"Two thousand!" called a voice from the covered stand.

"Three!" yelled another.

Nazim was beside himself with joy. "Stand straight, suck in your belly, turn your hip out," he instructed under his breath. "Noble sirs!" he cried out in mock anguish moving to the edge of the platform. "You can't expect me to let this beauty go for a mere three thousand denier!"

"Four then," shouted another, "and I want a paper from the physician."

The crowd laughed.

"Four," said Nazim. "Do I hear five?"

"Ten!" a deep bass voice rumbled over the heads of the crowd.

All eyes turned toward the massive, bloated figure reclining on soft cushions amongst the moneyed traders.

Nazim bowed deeply. "Sold to Belgutai, esteemed vizier to the Great Khan himself," he announced reverently, knowing there would be no further bids.

With the wave of a hand, on which gold rings and jewels had sunk into the putty-soft flesh of his swollen fingers, Belgutai idly acknowledged the sale.

†

Hsuan Tsang was meticulous in his preparations for an audience with the Great Khan. Scented baths had to be taken and ceremonial robes unpacked and put on. Although the merchant was nominally a prisoner of the Kuruk he nevertheless resided in a spacious yurt and was attended by a troop of hired servants. Those retainers fussed about him now, combing out his oiled hair and arranging the expensive robes. Tsang liked to be pampered and his wealth ensured him a certain degree of comfort, even in his present situation.

"Enough, enough!" He fluttered his hands at the attendants, who backed away. Standing before a mirror of silvered metal, he turned this way and that, admiring his imposing reflection.

†

Kuda stood outside Tsang's abode, waiting to escort the merchant through the encampment to the Great Khan's yurt. All around him, camp life went on as normal; children collected dung for the cooking fires while women stirred pots of boiling millet. Beyond the occasional glower from a passing warrior, nobody took any notice of him. Everybody believed he had accepted the role of Tsang's bodyguard and, like a good slave, was tamely submitting to his fate. In truth, his patience was wearing thin after weeks of playacting. Yet, it was necessary to continue with the charade, he told himself for the thousandth time. As Tsang's bodyguard, he was free to leave this place with the merchant and journey to Khorrassa. There, he would waste no time in extorting whatever back payment he deemed fit to purchase a fast horse, giving him the means to finally leave these accursed steppes far behind.

A good plan, he mused to himself, but for one thing. His face tightened with frustration when he thought upon it. The girl. She had saved his life and he was in her debt. It was an iron law of his northern clan that such a debt must be repaid. Engrained deeply within him was a barbaric code of honor that would not allow him to abandon her to a life of misery amongst these goat-herding tribesmen. He had to secure her freedom.

Tsang emerged from his yurt in a swirl of formal robes shimmering with traceries of silver thread.Sniffing the air, he grimaced and paused to raise a scented bag to his nose. The smell of unwashed bodies and human ordure was strong around the camp. Stepping gingerly, taking care not to disturb his hair, which was curled, greased and elaborately piled up on his head, he climbed into the sedan chair that awaited him. The alleyways that wound through the encampment had been churned to mud by the comings and goings of people, horses and wagons. Tsang would be transported over the mire by two burly retainers. Making himself comfortable, the merchant signaled for them to proceed. The servants raised the chair and set off at a brisk walk. An unsmiling Kuda followed close behind, hand on hilt.

In this fashion the tiny procession wound its way between hide tents until they reached a large, cleared space. A white felt yurt stood at the center of the open ground, twice as wide and half as high again as the homes of the people that surrounded it. It was an enormous construction, one so heavy that the cart that had brought it to that place had to be drawn by four mammoths, those great hairy elephants of the steppe. Guards in weather-beaten leathern armor strode forward, signing for the sedan chair to halt. An officer, a lean, grizzled fellow with a horseman's bow legs, approached them. Tsang, awkward in his bulky robes, clambered out of the chair to speak with him.

The audience with the Khan had been arranged months before. As the merchant was expected, after a few words with the officer, Tsang was led into the Khan's presence. Not knowing what else to do, Kuda followed and entered the imposing structure.

✝

The Great Khan sat squarely on a black marble throne, as solid and unmoving as if he himself were part of the marble. His feet, in cloth-of-gold boots with black spurs, were spread slightly apart. His hands rested on the arms of the throne and his slanted eyes were fixed on the three men approaching him.

He was a good six inches shorter than Kuda, but must have been nearly as heavy. All of that weight was bone and muscle. Kuda could see this clearly. The Khan wore black trousers with a gold sash. Above the waist, he wore an embroidered red vest that left most of his massive torso visible. His tanned and weathered olive-brown skin was seamed and corded with a warrior's muscle and a warrior's collection of scars. His head was shaved completely above the eyebrows, except for a long, black scalp-lock caught up in a silver ring. The Khan's bare skull gleamed so brightly that Kuda thought that it might have been waxed to give it that high polish.

On one side of the throne leaned a long, curved saber in a jeweled scabbard, within easy reach of the man's right hand. Against the other side leaned an unstrung bow of horn and ivory. Three curved daggers were stuck in his sash. He looked well equipped to deal with any armed opponent, ready to turn from Great Khan to warrior in the blink of an eye.

His warlords stood as motionless as statues about the yurt, eyeing the newcomers. Their faces flat and sallow, their eyes black as pitch and chillingly cruel.

The officer strode confidently toward the throne. Tsang fell into line behind him, with Kuda bringing up the rear. Twenty feet from the throne, they stopped, spread out and prostrated themselves on the carpet strewn floor. Kuda was only seconds behind the other two men in going down on his face.

The Khan's sharp eyes caught Kuda's slight hesitation. A chill, harsh voice rang out. "Who is this clumsy fool who knows not the proper forms of obeisance to us? And why are you, Hsuan Tsang, representative of the merchant's guild, so unwise as to bring him before us at a time when you should make all efforts to please me?"

The merchant quivered. Without raising his head, he spoke quickly. His words were muffled and distorted by his chin pressing against the thick rugs. "This man is from the fabled Northlands. A captive of your brave riders, until I bought him at auction to serve as my body guard."

The Khan made an impatient gesture with his left hand. "Answer my question, you simpering idiot! Before I strike your head from your shoulders!"

Tsang visibly winced at those last words. Kuda felt a sensation like a hundred thousand ants with very cold feet marching up and down his spine. There was deadly danger in this place, danger for them both. The Khan seemed not just bloodthirsty, whimsical, and tyrannical, but mad, or close enough to it to be a constant threat to those for whom his lightest word or whim meant life or death.

"I thought his rarity would prove a novelty for your magnificence," Tsang stammered. "His strength is prodigious, and Northern clansmen are so seldom seen outside of their own land."

A long silence descended upon the room like a weight. Kuda could almost feel it pressing him against the floor. He was finding it hard to breathe.

The silence continued. Suddenly, the Khan clapped both hands together, which, after the silence, sounded like a crash of thunder. "On your feet, all of you!"

The three men sprang up.

"You say he is strong?"

"I have never seen stronger," Tsang answered nervously.

The Khan gave a dismissive snort. "We shall see. Toht!"

At the snapped order a giant of a man, naked except for a loincloth, ducked through the yurt's entrance and plodded toward the throne. He was well over six and a half feet tall, yet still broad enough to appear squat. His upper arms were the size of an ordinary man's thighs. The giant stopped before the Khan and bobbed an egg-smooth head. Eyeing Kuda nastily, the newcomer folded huge, knotted arms across his ape-like chest and waited.

"This is Toht," the Khan announced with evident approval. "My champion wrestler. I have seen him break the necks of oxen with his bare hands! He will wrestle with your Northman. They will fight to the death, and we will see who is stronger." Suddenly, full of enthusiasm, the Khan called for a skin of airag — an alcoholic spirit made from fermented mare's milk. "If the bout pleases me merchant, you will be permitted to discuss your ransom and the opening of the trade routes with my councilors."

Tsang bowed deeply. "Your Magnificence is gracious beyond my poor deserts," he intoned, before backing away.

The two fighters turned to face each other. Toht's yellow face was as flat as a plate, with a hideous nose spread across it, a slit of a mouth, and two black button eyes that bored into Kuda. Kuda returned the gaze steadily, his face giving nothing away as, fumbling with buckles and fastenings, he loosened his weapon harness and let it clatter to the ground. Stepping out of it, he pulled the iron-scaled leather jerkin he wore over his head and flung it to one side. His muscled torso gleamed with a sheen of light perspiration. Glancing toward the throne, his heart lurched when he saw the slim figure veiled in clinging silks. It was the girl who had been haunting his dreams. She was presenting a fat skin of airag to the Khan.

Kuda's mouth set into a hard line when the Khan reached out and took the girl by the chin, raising her face to his. A tremulous half smile spread across her lovely, tilting mouth as she returned the Khan's stare. Kuda remembered her pale, lovely face floating over him in the darkness of the wagon and his chest tightened. Turning her head, she looked straight at him. Her eyes flew wide and all the color drained from her face. The Khan's eyes immediately flicked toward the barbarian, before returning to the girl, who looked back at her master with a blank, slightly nervous expression. Kuda stood mesmerized by her. He was totally unprepared when Toht threw himself forward.

✝

Recovering quickly from the shock of seeing the barbarian again, especially here, the last place she had ever expected to see him, Esmira moved away from the throne to stand and look disdainfully down her nose at him. Once again, she felt his hot gaze appraising her body. How dare the great clod stare at her like that! What did he want from her? Had the Khan noticed him gawping at her like a village half-wit? If he had, what would he think? She had been sold into the Khan's household as a virgin handmaiden and was prized as such. She was treated well and her duties were light. The Khan looked upon her favorably and she had hopes that he would soon take her as one of his wives. Now, here was this Northern ape leering at her in the Khan's presence, as though he were her long lost lover! She almost cried out with delight when Toht pounced.

†

Kuda gasped, winded, as he thumped down onto his back. He rolled to one side narrowly avoiding the large foot that stamped down at him. Springing to his feet, he leapt away and began circling left. Toht moved in the opposite direction, arms spread wide. As though responding to a silent cue the two men crashed together, their legs and hands moving swiftly to take and break grips. The match became a test of stamina as they heaved and sweated, long red marks appearing on their skin.

The excited warlords urged Toht on with bellows of unheeded advice. Between deep draughts of airag, the Khan also called out encouragement to his champion. Esmira stood in silence beside the throne, feeling nothing but revulsion at the sight of the two struggling men.

Grinning, Toht broke his grip and scuttled back. He had the measure of this outlander now. He was strong, maybe stronger than anybody he had ever faced before, but he had no technique. He decided he would break the slave's limbs one by one, then force him to drag his broken carcass to the foot of the throne to lick the Khan's boots. He knew that would please his master and earn him rich rewards. Rolling his bull neck, he stepped forward eagerly, arms flexing to grapple his opponent.

Kuda did not fear the giant but he hated his arrogance. That, coupled with the whippings, imprisonment and weeks of humiliating slavery, made him furious. His rage broke its bounds, as though it were some terrible black animal over which he had no control. He lunged at the Khan's champion.

The two men collided in a bone crunching smack of flesh. Using his superior technique, Toht fought to assert himself. But he may as well have been attempting to wrestle a maddened tiger. Snapping his head forward, Kuda locked his jaws on Toht's nose, causing the giant to thrash and flail at Kuda with his fists. Kuda rode the struggles, all the while grinding and slicing and gripping with his teeth. Suddenly, his teeth met within the gristle and hot blood flooded his mouth. He pulled his head back sharply, tearing away a mouth full of shredded flesh. Toht staggered back, slapping a hand to the gore-filled hole in his face as he fell to his knees. Kuda, spitting gobbets of red flesh onto the rich carpets, quickly stepped around behind the kneeling man. His hands shot out to clamp onto the sides of the giant's head. The wrestler tried to duck away but his skull was held in a vice. Kuda hunched his enormous shoulder muscles, and leaning back, began to twist. Curling his hands into fists Toht abandoned technique and began hammering awkwardly at his opponent. He screamed as his head was twisted back past his shoulder. The muscles in Kuda's arms writhed with effort. The gathered warlords were silent now, their faces set in stone. Toht's eyes, bulging inhumanly large, were filled with the desperate knowledge of his own death. The giants' spine snapped with a noise like that of a stick breaking. His dying scream cut off in an instant. For a second, his head stared sightlessly backward, then Kuda released him and, as the twisted neck grotesquely righted itself, the man collapsed. Straightening up, the barbarian laughed, a sudden, fierce burst of joy that had something animal about it.Contemptuously, he kicked at the corpse before bending to retrieve his weapons

The watching Kuruk were silent for a long second. Then, as one, they began to cheer. Tsang's heart resumed beating when, to his surprise, the Khan smiled and beckoned him forward.

"You spoke the truth, merchant. That was rare sport. I never thought to see Toht bested. You may carry out your negotiations."

The trader bowed his head graciously and the Khan waved him away.

FOUR

Kuda strolled through the camp with no specific destination in mind. He had a lot of spare time on his hands. His duties as Tsang's bodyguard were non-existent; the merchant was in no danger now that it was common knowledge that the Khan had smiled upon him. The perfumed trader spent most of his day closeted away with the Khan's secretaries, hammering out a deal to keep the trade routes open. This meant that, once he had escorted Tsang to the meetings, Kuda was free to do as he pleased. He wandered the camp, his mind preoccupied with half-formed schemes to free the girl, Esmira. The vision of her beauty and kindness stayed with him, always there in the recesses of his mind, yet coming to the fore at unexpected moments. He thought about the way she had cared for him in the back of the wagon, the gentle touch of her hands. Kuda had learnt her name from Tsang, but when he insisted the merchant buy her so that she could leave with them, the Khorrasian trader had recoiled in horror.

"It is out of the question," Tsang had whispered. "She belongs to the Khan now, and is beyond our help. Forget her. You may as well wish for the stars. Sate your lust with the harlots who ply their trade amongst the market stalls. I will provide you with gold enough."

"You do not understand. How could you?" Kuda snapped back, without elaborating.

"Do not torture yourself unduly," Tsang sniffed. "I realize she is beautiful, but she is hardly unique. Anyway, prettiness isn't always a gift in a woman, especially if they own a mirror."

He scowled as he recalled Tsang's words. The merchant would not help him, but, he told himself, what did a venal, preening ninny like Tsang know of women and honor, anyway. For Kuda, there was no choice in the matter of honor. The moment a clansman forsakes that code, then all is lost, for even though he forgets on one occasion, it is the beginning of the end. Bit by bit, the code will be qualified and any break with it justified, until he is no longer a man. So Kuda amused himself as best as he could, spending his time and Tsang's money on the camp women who, between bouts of carnal activity, gradually taught him the Kuruk tongue.

He also passed the long hours of inactivity aimlessly wandering the streets of yurts. A miniature town made of felt and hide within whose walls were played out all the tragedies and dramas of any community; births and deaths, family life, love and loneliness. During the course of yet another long aimless wander, Kuda was plodding between the domed tents when he looked up to find himself standing before the Ziggurat. His footsteps halted at the edge of the open, circular space that surrounded the weather-beaten and grim structure. Nothing grew in that circle and nobody walked upon the bare ground that looked cracked and blackened, as though it had been scorched by a grass fire. The place radiated an eerie stillness and Kuda shifted uneasily. He placed a booted foot inside the circle and withdrew it quickly when he felt heat striking up through his leather sole. He recalled Stul's wild tales of a dragon slumbering beneath the ground and made a sign against evil. Lifting his eyes to the peak of the pyramid, he regarded the weirdly designed temple that squatted there and wondered about the Ziggurrat's sole occupant. He'd been told that the creature was only ever glimpsed when the Khan ascended the steps to commune with it. He shuddered at the idea of an unholy tryst between some demonical being who controlled a dragon and the mad Khan.

"Sorcery," he breathed. The word shivered through him like an icy breath. With undue haste, he turned on his heel to quickly lose himself amongst the domed yurts.

✝

Hand trembling in an iron grip, the muscles of his arm locked into tight knots, Kuda bore inexorably down on his opponent's rigid forearm. The tribesmen crowding around the trestle table roared encouragement at the straining pair. Apart from an occasional hiss escaping through gritted teeth, the two struggling men remained silent for they had no breath to spare. Spittle spattered upon Kuda's skin. His adversary's lumpish face was only inches away from his. In the flickering, hissing light of mutton-fat lamps, grease-balls of sweat glistened from the man's honeycomb of open pores, and his tiny pig eyes glinted malevolently. Locking his enormous shoulder muscles, Kuda exerted all his strength. The back of his opponent's hand thudded down onto the table top. The man let out a strangled cry and quickly twisted his body to prevent his shoulder being dislocated.

A moan of dismay rose from the semi-circle of warriors. Kuda stood up from the table, smothering a smile. His opponent also stood, rubbing his arm and grinning ruefully at his comrades as they patted him on the back.

The steppe-riders were a strange breed, Kuda mused to himself, glancing around the table. They were constantly challenging him to arm-wrestling matches and did not mind being beaten time and time again. He could not imagine his Northern clansmen ever allowing such a display. The humiliation would have been too much for them. Even so, he was careful not to celebrate his victories. He knew it was dangerous to antagonize or humiliate them. Their goodwill and respect would be more valuable than their hatred and resentment.

Turning aside exhortations for another match, he moved off to seat himself at another table where he called for a mug of airag. The tables were set up every night in the market place by stallholders who peddled potent alcoholic brews to warriors who felt the need to get away from their wives and children for a few hours every evening. The crowd tonight was roaring and boisterous but, nevertheless, good-natured, with only the occasional fist-fight breaking out. The Khan's law forbade the carrying of edged weapons to drinking dens and those laws were adhered to. Any breach of them was a matter for the Master of Punishment, who was well known for his ruthlessness.

A figure dropped down onto the bench opposite Kuda. It was Gutchluk, a dour-faced, lean and leathery warrior who held the rank of Orkhon, a commander of fifty. "Our young men never tire of trying their strength with you Northman," he remarked.

"It is the way of young men," Kuda agreed, taking a deep swallow of his drink.

"Take care not to break any sword arms. The Khan will have need of them during the forthcoming campaign season."

Kuda's ears pricked up at the mention of the coming campaigns. "And where will the Great Khan lead the horde this summer?" he asked.

"Who knows?" Gutchluk shrugged. "It is only known that the Kha Khan will call a meeting of his warlords after he has visited the Ziggurat one last time." The Orkhon leaned closer, dropping his voice to slightly above a whisper. "Rumor has it that the dragon keeper requires one more tear from the Gods before he unleashes his beast to our service. So, before we can escape from this accursed place we wait upon yet another shooting star."

Kuda frowned. "It seems to me that you would be wiser to let sleeping dragons lie. What need have the Kuruk of such a creature when you already have a mighty horde straining to be unleashed?"

"I agree!" Gutchluk grinned suddenly. "You speak a lot of good sense for a barbarian, Kuda." He sighed heavily. "But we are just simple warriors, you and I, and there is a lot of politics involved nowadays." He belched and eased back on the bench. "That scented fop who bought you could probably tell you more about the Khan's plans than I can."

A one-stringed fiddle struck up somewhere in the growing darkness and a minstrel began to sing. His voice was soon drowned out by drunken revelers, who insisted on joining in on the chorus. Kuda had to raise his voice to be heard. "I am no slave, Gutchluk. Is there not room for me in this horde?"

The Orkhon regarded him seriously. "I do not doubt that you are a mighty warrior, Kuda, but you could not fight as we do. Our children can ride before they learn to walk. It takes years to master the accurate shooting of a bow from the saddle. Our squadrons are swift and maneuverable, and our enemies can never come to grips with us before we encircle and destroy them." He shook his head. "If this were normal times, you could have come with us to toil at the siege works that we build whenever we encounter a walled city. But this season, with a dragon at our head, what need have we for siege works?"

Kuda, struggling to control his temper, drained his tankard and, without another word, rose and walked away from the table. Gutchluk's good-natured laughter rang in his ears. "Your strength is legendary, but we have seen you ride. You sit a saddle like a sack of millet tied in the middle."

✝

Two nights later, Kuda stood relieving himself against a rock out on the open steppe. He was on his way back to the camp after having spent the evening watching horse races and drinking airag. As he shook himself dry, he blearily noticed that everyone else on the road around him had stopped in their tracks to silently stare up at the heavens. He followed their gaze just in time to see an object streaking across the night sky. A pulsating green light leaving behind it a lingering trail of smoke as it dipped towards the misty horizon. His eyes followed the object's fiery course to its conclusion, watching as it crashed amongst far mountains to be consumed in its own explosive brilliance. The Gods had cried again it seemed.

✝

The Khan's face was set and unreadable as he set off alone across the bare, open space before the Ziggurat. He strode along purposefully under the gaze of the entire Kuruk nation who pressed as close as they dared about the perimeter of scorched earth. Reaching the base of the pyramidal structure, the Khan began climbing the flight of steps that led up its steep face.

From the midst of the silent crowd, Kuda watched the lonely figure ascending the giant steps. He shook his head slowly. The Khan was definitely mad, he concluded. Who else but a madman would walk into the den of a demon, who was also a master of dragons?

There was movement at the top of the steps. The ring of spectators recoiled in horror as a monstrous apparition stepped into view. It moved like some strange, angular bird of prey, a vulture that walked on long, spindly legs. The creature stood at the top of the steps like a tall, skinny spider, its long body swathed in pale grey robes that rippled in the breeze. Its skull was bare and bleached white as bone.

Its huge, unblinking eyes seemed to be watching the man climbing toward it. Not a sound came from the horde of people watching. Every one of them seemed to be holding their breath.

The Khan pulled himself up the final step to stand before the tall, hunched being. The pair stood facing each other for a long moment before the keeper nodded in nonhuman approval and turned away to lead the Khan into the temple that crouched behind them. As they disappeared from view, the paralysis that had gripped the mob melted away and murmurings of disquiet rippled through the crowd. Nevertheless, despite the mutterings, people began to disperse peacefully. Pushing his way through the jostling mass of smelly tribespeople, Kuda made his way across the camp to the slave pits.

†

Standing before the metal grille he knew so well, Kuda peered into the gloom beyond the bars.

"Stul!" he shouted. "Are you there?"

A short figure detached itself from the shadows to shuffle up to the bars. Stul, with a crooked grin upon his face, squinted up through the grille. "Kuda! You have come to visit your old friend. Did you miss me?"

"My life has become so silent and peaceful that I thought I had gone deaf. So, I came back to make sure my ears still work and, unfortunately, it seems they do."

The short tribesman puffed out his chest. "I am top dog here now. Everybody respects me and pays heed to the wisdom I impart daily. Why, just the other …"

Kuda cut him off. "Did you see the shooting star?"

"Yes. What I could of it from this hole," Stul answered, nonplussed.

"It landed in the mountains west of here. Do you know that range?"

"Of course! You are talking of the Blue Mountains. My homeland. No-one knows those peaks better than me. I am famed among my people as ..."

"Enough!" Kuda made a chopping motion with his hand. "You had better be right, you little braggart, because you are taking me there," he snapped sharply, before turning away. "Once I find that swindler, Nazim, I'll buy you."

Stul's eyes widened in surprise. "You have gold enough?"

"Gold, pah! A few coppers should suffice. Though, having your tongue cut out will cost me another silver piece," Kuda growled, hiding a smile. "But that's money well spent."

FIVE

On a bright misty dawn, with the sun barely showing in the east, the Kuruk nation began to move. The Khan's marshals and warlords led the tribes into the west, while Hsuan Tsang, a former prisoner, led his small caravan in the opposite direction.

Side by side, Kuda and Stul sat their mounts on a rise of ground, taking in the spectacle of the vast horde streaming away across the steppe. As far as the eye could see, the grasslands were covered by a jostling carpet of men and beasts. As well as a quarter of a million warriors, half a million ponies had to be herded, with as many sheep, goats, yaks, camel and oxen. The need for grazing land was such that the horde could only remain in one place for a month at a time. The nation's progress would be marked by a wide swathe of newly created semi-desert.

Surrounded by the herds, a seemingly endless column of ox-drawn carts crawled across the steppe, with the huddled figures of women and young children on them. Following the families' wagons were more heavily laden carts piled high with the felt and wood of dismantled yurts. Even from this distance, they could hear the squealing and groaning of the huge solid wheels turning on wooden axles, and the occasional crack of a whip.

Kuda focused an intent gaze upon the cart lines, hoping to catch a glimpse of the girl, Esmira, but the rising dust clouds frustrated him. With a curse, he tugged his pony's head around and urged it into a trot away from the horde and towards Tsang's small caravan of traveler's that was snaking its way across the steppe in the opposite direction.

†

Hsuan Tsang lounged on silken cushions while a servant softly combed out his hair and applied scented oil to the long strands. The trade legate sighed contentedly, allowing the nervous tension that had been his constant companion over the past few months, flow out of him. Suddenly, a massive form ducked through the yurt's low entranceway. Tsang jumped at the unexpected intrusion and let out a yelp.

"I really do wish you would learn to knock Kuda!" he snapped waspishly.

Ignoring the merchant, the big barbarian crossed to the bubbling pot that hung over the tent's central fire. His belly rumbled as the delicious aroma of marmot and wild onion stew filled his nostrils. Grabbing an empty bowl, he began helping himself. Squatting down opposite Tsang, he began shoveling the tender meat into his mouth.

"Tell me what the Khan is planning," he demanded between mouthfuls.

Pretending not to notice his bodyguard's table manners, Tsang cleared his throat delicately before he began speaking with relish. He enjoyed spreading gossip. "The Kha Khan has decreed that the nation begin their march to the west while he remains at the Ziggurat."

"That makes no sense," Kuda slurped. "Will he allow his generals to make war without him? To reap all the spoils and glory while he sits doing nothing? The Khan might be mad, but he is still a warrior."

"Indeed he is," the merchant nodded sagely. "Which is why he has commanded his warlords not to carry out any offensives until he has joined them. He ..." Tsang paused in mid flow to glance dramatically around the yurt, as though suspecting a spy to be lurking behind every cushion. "He plans to join them by riding upon the back of a dragon. In a single night, he will be carried across leagues of steppe to the head of his armies."

TEARS OF THE GODS

"Dragon!" Kuda snorted in disbelief and threw his empty bowl to the floor. "If there were such a beast, why does he not ride it now? The campaign season has begun. What is he waiting for?"

Tsang tut-tutted and tossed Kuda a cloth to wipe his mouth with before continuing. "The keeper will not release the dragon to do the Khan's bidding until the Khan has presented him with the final tear of the Gods. You yourself saw that tear falling. The Khan has already dispatched his divisions to secure the star-rock and bring it back to the Ziggurat."

"It landed in the Blue Mountains," Kuda said, reaching for a bulging skin of airag. "The Khan's men will find it hard going there."

"Undoubtedly," Tsang shrugged. "But they will persevere. In any event, it is no concern of ours. My negotiations were successful, which means that the trading routes to the west will remain open. Caravans will flow across the steppe carrying the riches of the world from city to city completely unmolested." He rubbed his hands together. "The golden city of Khorrassa will grow ever richer." He smiled indulgently at the Northman. "I'm sure you will find my city to your taste."

Kuda raised the skin up to his face and squirted out a long draught into his mouth before wiping his lips with the back of his hand. "I am not going to Khorrassa," he stated matter-of-factly.

Tsang started again and this time the servant yelped.

"What do you mean? Not going!" he spluttered. "You are my slave. You must do as I say. I paid good money for you!"

Kuda paused to savor the warm glow of the alcoholic spirit spreading throughout his chest before answering. "I am journeying to the Blue Mountains," he said, lowering the skin.

Slapping the servant's fussing hands away, Tsang shuffled forward on the cushions, clearly anxious. "Allow me to explain slavery to you. It is a concept I think you have trouble with." He took a deep breath. "You are my property. You belong to me. You must do exactly as I say at all times until I either free you or sell you on."

Kuda smacked his lips. "So free me then if it makes you feel better."

"I have not finished with your services yet," Tsang shrieked indignantly. Storming to his feet, he pointed an accusing finger at the barbarian. "It's that slave-girl, isn't it? Esmira. The one the Khan has just taken as one of his wives. I see your plan, it's as plain as the broken nose on your face. You're going to try and find that star-stone before the Khan's men do, then use it to bargain for the girl's freedom. Am I wrong?"

"You are not wrong," Kuda nodded.

"I knew it!" Tsang exclaimed in bitter triumph. "That's why you are dragging that obnoxious hillman around with you. To guide you through the mountains!" Flicking unbound hair out of his face, the effeminate merchant drew himself up to his full height. "I will simply not allow it. I forbid you to go."

"Who will stop me?" Kuda smiled thinly, indicating Tsang's manservant, who cowered amongst the cushions. "Your hairdresser?"

Tsang stood rigid, searching for words. "The girl is not worth it, Kuda. Believe me, you are making a mistake. Also, the hill tribes are not to be trusted. They will slit your throat before you even glimpse the star-stone. Besides, even if, by some miracle, you do obtain it, the Khan would never strike a deal with you."

"I hear you," Kuda said, rising to his feet. "But I owe her more than sits comfortably with me. It is a burden. A debt to be repaid. You do not need my protection on this journey for you travel under the Khan's mandate. No-one will dare impede you. I will leave when I am ready."

Without another word, the huge outlander swung away and ducked out of the yurt.

Tsang hung his head. "You repay your debt to the wrong person Kuda," he whispered sadly. "Though you would never believe that."

†

Uracc rode at the head of a compact column of prime, battle-hardened warriors. They were all of the Claw tribe, skilled at murder and lacking any shred of conscience. Along with scores of other squadrons, they had been ordered to the Blue Mountains to seek out the star-stone. This, Uracc would do, but he had other business to take care of first. He was well pleased with the men he led, for, though they traveled under the Khan's directive, they had not questioned him when he had ordered a small deviation from those orders.

†

The encampment was in chaos when Tsang ducked out of his yurt. Dawn was coming, but torches had been lit, spreading a greasy, yellow light that revealed running figures. Mounted warriors milled around raising dust and confusion.

"What is the meaning of this?" he shouted into the melee of darting shadowy forms.

The whinnying of horses and the shouts of the warriors continued, but a group of horsemen swung around to face him. Tsang saw that the raiders were bondsmen of the Khan, grim and dark in their boiled leather armor.

The dominant horseman spat a question at him. "Where is the barbarian?"

Tsang paled slightly but his face remained impassive. "This caravan travels under the protection of the Kha Khan. You are risking his wrath by even being here."

The young, well-built rider seemed to find Tsang's response irritating. "Hand him over merchant, or leave your bones here. If you force our hand we will leave no-one alive to carry tales to the Khan."

Sensing the deep-seated malice behind the rider's words, Tsang allowed himself a brief nod before answering. "Two nights ago, the outlander slave you speak of stole some ponies and escaped. I decided not to delay the entire caravan in a fruitless search for him." He spread his hands expansively. "Our camp is not large and you have many men. If you cannot find him here, that proves the truth of my words."

Glancing sourly about him, Uracc let out a string of oaths. He felt a sick sense of disappointment, for he had been anticipating Kuda's death with great expectation.

†

A grey wolf sat on its haunches watching the horses passing by. Tongue lolling, it made no move to pursue them. All around, the grass grew green and lush, moving with the perpetual winds that scoured the exposed plain. It was early spring and game was plentiful. Deer, marmots, foxes, wild dogs and a thousand other small animals. So the wolf, unwilling to exert himself unduly, dismissed the horses to flop down onto its full belly.

The two specks of humanity rode across a place of enormousness. A huge sky. Huge mountains. Kuda, riding a bay mare that cantered across the plain in a tireless rhythm, wore a padded deel that left his muscular arms bare, revealing a web of pale scars. His leggings that gripped the mare's flanks were made of hard wearing leather, as were the soft boots in the stirrups. A long, heavy saber thumped against his back with each thrust of the pony beneath him and a hide bowcase rested behind his thigh. Behind him, carrying canteens of water and packs of provisions, he trailed a second pony on a lead line. A little way off, Stul kept pace on his own mare. Another pony was tied to his saddle horn, laden with packs containing nose bags for the horses and a cooking pot for the men. The laden ponies also carried axes and ropes, shields, fur-trimmed helmets and sheaves of arrows. The ponies, who still bore their winter coats, were strong steppe-bred beasts that could run like the wind all day long.

As they progressed, the silence of the land settled gently upon them, a silence not broken but somehow heightened by the sound of creaking leather and snorting horses. But the loneliness could not blunt Kuda's sense of excitement; each mile covered, each successive camp along the way, added to his sense of freedom. With the breeze fanning his mane of coarse black hair out behind him, he drew the clean fresh air of the open steppe deep into his lungs with relish. Each mile increased his sense of well-being. They traveled in daylight, bedding down before the sun slipped from sight behind the western mountain range, and rising just as it was making a reappearance in the east. Day by day, the outlines of the distant mountains began to harden.

†

In the evenings, by the glowing dung fire, Kuda had no choice but to listen to Stul's endless prattling and bragging as he sat watching the setting sun turn the mountains to fire. Although, this was a small price to pay for the sense of optimism and health the journey had bestowed upon him.

Feelings all the more intense for the period of miserable slavery through which he had come.

One evening, Stul interrupted his flow of usual nonsense to ask a question. "You have not told me yet why we are traveling to the Blue Mountains."

Chewing on a mouthful of smoke-cured meat, Kuda looked up to regard the rascally mountain man. After swallowing and sucking his teeth for a long minute he answered. "We are seeking the star-stone that fell there."

Stul's eyebrows lifted. "What do you want with a God's tear?"

"That's my business. Yours is to lead me to it."

Stul shook his head dejectedly. "The mountains are vast. No doubt the Khan has already dispatched many riders to find it. What makes you think we can beat them to it?"

Kuda helped himself to more meat and answered with a question of his own. "What do the hill tribes do when they see the Kuruk approach?"

"They withdraw into the high passes."

"What will they do when they see us approach?"

"Stick us with arrows and steal our horses," Stul answered, as though it were obvious.

"But I thought you were an important man amongst the mountain people," said Kuda, around another mouthful of meat. "A chieftain of your tribe. Famous for your deeds!"

"So I am!" the short man snapped back, squaring his shoulders.

"So, when they recognize you for the famous slayer that you are, they will stay their hand. Then you can talk to them," Kuda went on reasonably. "They would have seen the God's tear fall into the mountains. They can point us in the right direction, thus giving us an advantage over the Khan's men."

Stul frowned worriedly. "The Khan's forces will also have scouts and …"

He broke off and leapt to his feet with a sharp cry of alarm. "Look there, Kuda! Look! Now do you believe me?" He pointed a trembling finger out over the steppe.

Kuda whipped around to see a half-visible shape, a darker form against the already dark sky. It came at an unnatural speed, flying low over the plain. Indistinct in the twilight, it was moving as fast as an arrow shot from a bow.

"What in the seven hells is that?" he hissed.

"Dragon," shrieked Stul.

As they watched, the dark silhouette changed shape and the glowing coals of eyes swiveled toward them. The hobbled ponies whickered nervously.

"It sees us!" screamed Stul, leaping to stamp out the fire.

Kuda was standing stock-still, rooted to the spot, the hairs on the back of his neck bristling. "It makes no sound," he whispered to himself.

As he watched, the thing seemed to pulsate with a flickering light before shooting upward faster than their eyes could follow.

Kuda, his face now set in grim lines, moved slowly past Stul, who had his face pressed to the ground. Curling his fingers around the worn hilt of his saber, he hefted it in his hand. He stood motionless, while, all around, the stygian gloom of the steppe deepened swiftly into true night.

"I told you there are dragons," Stul's muffled voice sounded behind him. "You saw it."

Kuda made a non-committal grunt. "I don't know what I saw. Now get your face out of the dirt. We need to move camp."

†

It was mid-morning when he spotted the moving specks of riders in the far distance. Narrowing his eyes, he watched them, hoping they were not following. His mouth set into a firm line when he saw the riders turn, and he noted the rise of dust as they kicked their mounts into a gallop. Kuda looked around. Behind him and on each side, the grassland rolled away as far as the eye could see. Ahead of them rose the mountains, their jagged peaks covered in a mantle of snow that shone in the spring sunlight. The nearest foothills were only half a day's ride away. They would be pushed to lose the riders in this open land, but possible if only they could reach the hills. He started his mare galloping, pleased that she was strong and well rested. Perhaps the trailing men's horses would be tired, and they could increase the distance between them.

Stul glanced over his shoulder when Kuda pounded past him. What he saw made him also dig in his heels. They galloped side by side in silence. Kuda's eyes traveled feverishly along the hills, seeing the lightly-forested slopes. The stunted pines were spread too thin to hide in, he thought. With irritation growing deep in his chest, he rode on. Looking back, he noticed the riders were closing in. There were twenty of them in pursuit. Their blood would be up for the chase, he knew. They would be excited and yelling, though their cries were lost far behind in the distance. He bared his teeth to the wind as he rode. Under his padded jerkin, the shirt of chain mail he wore was a comforting weight, as was the long saber slapping against his back. If they pressed him he would butcher the lot of them, he told himself. He would not become a slave again. They would pay dearly for his skin.

✝

As they drew closer to the rising ground, the landscape became a dreary succession of barren hills slashed by steep-sided ravines. Pulling his mare's head around, he headed for one of the shadowed canyons. Just before they plunged into the defile, Kuda glanced backward again. The riders were less than half a mile away now, stretched out in a line of advance a hundred yards wide. The defile was narrow and winding, and soon they were lost to sight from their pursuers. Here, the ground was bare of vegetation, and the track grew more and more stony, twisting and turning around the spurs of the hills. Kuda untied the lead rein of his packhorse from his saddle and threw it to Stul, who caught it deftly.

"Don't stop, keep going," he yelled at the mountain man.

For once Stul kept his mouth shut and, kicking in his heels, galloped the ponies onwards and deeper into the gulley. Kuda swerved his mount off the trail and pulled it to a stop on the other side of a great slab of tumbled rock. Hidden in the slot of rock, he turned his mount around in the confined space to face back the way he had entered. Leaning forward, he patted the mare's neck to keep her calm before drawing his bow from its case. Placing the bow's lower end in his left stirrup, he pressed down upon the upper end. The raw power in the recurved layers of horn and wood resisted his efforts. It took all his strength. Quickly, he looped the bowstrings noose about the upper nock. Plucking the tensed string, he gave a satisfied grunt and selected an arrow from the hunting quiver that hung from his saddle. Then he waited.

There was a sudden rush of hooves as the pursuers galloped past his hiding place. Kuda's eyes narrowed in puzzlement when he only counted five horses. Shrugging, he urged his horse forward and charged back out onto the trail. Falling in behind the last rider, he raced to catch him up. Ahead of him, the five pursuers were spread out, the strongest ponies their flanks lathered, soaked with sweat were pressing ahead in their eagerness to catch Stul. The riders, intent on their quarry, were completely unaware of Kuda gaining on them. The Northman's gaze was hard and relentless as he slapped the free end of his reins across the mare's neck. Steep rock walls whipped past in a blur of speed as the narrow gulley twisted and turned. Gripping with his knees, Kuda looped the reins around his saddle horn. With both hands free, he raised the bow. Drawing back the bowstring he aimed down the arrow's shaft. With the plunging of the pony beneath him, the arrow's head swung wildly, making it difficult to aim for the rider. So, he concentrated his aim on the horse, a larger target, and released the string.

The arrow buried itself up to its fletching in the horse's rump. Whinnying in shock and pain the animal reared, throwing its rider. Kuda rode down on the prostrate form without slackening his pace, letting the hooves of his steed hammer the man into the dirt. Coming swiftly up behind the next warrior, he shoved the bow back into its case before reaching back over one shoulder to slide his saber from its sheath. Drawing alongside the warrior, he urged his pony slightly ahead and hacked back with his blade. The sharp steel cut into the rider's face, splitting his head horizontally like a melon. There was an explosion of blood and teeth as the warrior flopped backwards out of the saddle. Kuda spurred his horse on. The next rider along the ravine had obviously sensed something amiss; he was twisting in his saddle, straining to look behind him. His eyes widened in shock at the sight of the giant Northman thundering down upon him, the bright steel in his fist scattering droplets of blood. Sawing at his reins, the man attempted to turn his mount by brute force to face the unexpected attack. The animal gave a whinny of protest and spun on its haunches, turning so that its front hooves were clawing on the loose gravel of the canyon wall as it tried to find a purchase. Kuda's steed barged full-tilt into the stalled horse. Both beasts went down in a bone-snapping tangle. Kuda's mare fell heavily but he was able to kick his feet out of the stirrups and jump clear. Rolling to his feet in a cloud of dust, he saw that the remaining pair of Kuruk were swinging their mounts back down the gulley, heading toward him. Even closer though, the fallen rider was staggering to his feet. Kuda charged. With the full weight of his run, he knocked the man back to the ground. Pinning the rider's head down with one foot, he placed the point of his blade on the back of the man's neck and leaned his full weight on it. The keen steel sank in to sever the rider's spine with the precision of a surgeon.

A horseman swept down upon him. Kuda gritted his teeth as he lowered himself into a crouch, hefted his blade and spread his feet wide. He swung his saber into the racing beast's forelegs, causing the horse to tumble headlong, catapulting its rider from the saddle. The rider hurtled through the air to dash his brains out on a rocky outcrop. The final rider pulled his mount down from full gallop on to its haunches, sprang from the saddle and rushed the barbarian. He swarmed in with a series of sweeps and thrusts, aiming for neck and belly. Kuda countered the clumsy attack. The sharp clash of blades echoed around the surrounding steep slopes. The Kuruk warrior snarled in frustration, his dark eyes locked on the Northman. Kuda pressed him back. Forcing the smaller man's blade lower, until he stamped one booted foot down on its bright length, trapping the steel against the ground. Keeping a tight hold on his weapon the Kuruk was yanked forward by this unexpected move to be skewered in the guts. Kuda twisted the blade and withdrew his saber in a burst of blood and dragging entrails. Clamping a hand to his midriff, the man dropped to his knees and began screaming. The barbarian's blade flashed in an executioner's stroke and the riders head jumped from his shoulders.

Alert to his surroundings again, Kuda's head jerked up at the clatter of horse's hooves echoing and re-echoing between the steep canyon walls. Someone was riding at speed down the ravine. He raised his sword just as Stul and the ponies burst into view.

"There are more of them behind me!" the hillman yelled, riding flat on the saddle as he sped past Kuda. "Half of them must have circled around to gain the higher ground. They were waiting in ambush."

Kuda barely had time to take in what Stul was saying before the panicking man had disappeared off down the trail, yipping to his mount as he went, urging the animal on. Slamming his saber home in its sheath he grabbed at his pony's head. Taking hold of rein and pommel, he vaulted to the horse's back and set off at a gallop.

†

Sprawled flat upon the ground until the sun went down and the wind turned cold and plaintive, they lay across their ponies' necks hidden from view by the tall grass. They camped out on the steppe that night, with the mountains standing up before them, sheer and black. Racing from the hills they had pushed the ponies for hours and the beasts were exhausted. Their recovering mounts were now stood a little way off, contentedly cropping at the sweet spring grass, their tails turned to the wind.

The men did not light a fire. Sitting on the soft grass relaxed and unworried, they chewed on dried meat and passed a skin of airag between them. It was a pitch-dark night and the chances of their pursuers coming across them on the open plain were astronomical.

Inevitably, Stul was the first to speak. "Do you know of any reason why the warriors of the Claw tribe would want you dead?" he asked conversationally.

Kuda shook his head.

"Did you murder one of their number?" the mountain man persisted.

"Not until today," Kuda responded shortly, before adding, "unless the Khan's wrestling champion was of their tribe."

"I doubt it. But even if he was, you killed him in a fair fight and there would be no grudge held against you for that. This is more serious." Stul looked thoughtful. "Blood vengeance, reproach or insult. Maybe you shamed one of them?"

"That is possible," admitted Kuda.

"I knew it," Stul pulled a face. "What happened?"

Kuda shrugged his yard-wide shoulders. "I disarmed a young man in front of his Father and ransomed him for a horse. When I was taken as a slave, he tried to beat me to death, but I flattened him under his own pony."

Stul looked at the big outlander in blank amazement for a long beat before muttering inadequately, "That would do it."

"Will they keep coming?" Kuda asked, sounding unconcerned.

"Yes. To the Kuruk, retribution is an obligation."

The barbarian's face took on a hard-edged expression. "Then, they are fools. I will kill them all."

Stul sighed heavily and shrugged. "Young warriors are not noted for their wisdom or their long memory for anything except insults." He held out a hand. "Pass the airag."

SIX

The next day, they resumed their journey, climbing steadily through the foothills. On the fourth day, they passed over the snow-line. The hooves made little sound on the snow as they climbed higher into the mountains where the eternal winds wailed around the peaks. The gales tore viciously at them, hurling stinging snow into their eyes and against any exposed skin. To Kuda's relief, Stul seemed to know every twist and turn of the mountainous pathway they were following. Over the next few days, the hillman led him confidently through every high pass and dangerous ford, so they wasted no time in searching for the right road, and journeyed swiftly.

At the start of their eighth day in the mountains Stul suddenly stiffened in his saddle and reined his pony to a halt. Ahead of them, like a string of dark beads against the snow, several figures were stood in a crescent straddling the path. Kuda walked his mount forward until he drew level with Stul.

"Keep your hands away from your weapons," Stul advised from the side of his mouth, clearly worried.

Kuda didn't respond but he noticed that his companions face had gone deathly white. He swept his gaze along the frieze of armed men straddling the path. Noting the filth that covered the heavy fur clothing the newcomers were bundled in, their bear grease matted long hair and thick beards, he felt a repugnance that made him shift in his saddle. Their cold eyes returned his gaze with a predatory intensity. Weapons held ready, the raggedly dressed strangers stood four-square. By the nature of their stance, it was clear they claimed this territory as their own. One of their number advanced, bellowing a challenge. He was a squat, thick-chested man with a face disfigured by battle.

Behind him, the mountain men brandished their weapons and began shouting insults and threats in their outlandish tongue.

"Hold my pony," Stul grunted.

Tossing his reins to Kuda, he slid from the saddle. With arms spread wide, he swaggered towards the bellowing figure.

Kuda was uncomfortable with this reversal of positions but he knew he had little choice but to trust the hillman. Resigned, he sat and watched impassively as Stul's verbal avalanche crushed any further words from the mountain men's leader. Feigning indifference, he turned his eyes to the sky. High above, two eagles were effortlessly circling, their outstretched wings motionless. Stul's raised voice continued on without a pause.

✝

The snow began to fall as the fifteen Kuruk warriors made camp in the lee of a vast cliff that soared into whiteness above their heads. They huddled miserably around the small fire they had managed to coax into life, though its feeble warmth did little to warm them. The mountains were a cold and hostile place that each of them knew only as a wilderness of poor hunting and sure death in winter. They were bone-tired from pushing hard to cut the escaped slave's trail over the past few days. Every peak they climbed was followed by a twisting valley and another strength-sapping climb to find the best path through. Adding to their discomfort was the knowledge that it was spring down upon the steppes and the Kuruk nation was riding to glory without them. Uracc's feud with the fugitive barbarian was something they could have done without, but they understood it. As his steppe brethren, they were obligated to help him. They understood that the outlander's death was the only way of expunging his shame. So, they kept their mouths shut and their eyes fixed on the flickering flames, each of them acutely aware of Uracc's sullen presence. He sat silently amongst them, his slitted eyes reflecting only the burning desire to exact retribution for the shame the foreigner had inflicted upon him.

✝

Kuda urged his pony upward. As it scrambled over loose rock and scree, he was forced to cling to the pommel. Ahead of him, Stul swayed in the saddle. Kuda eyed the back of the little man's head resentfully. "You did tell them that you were a famous warrior of the Blue Mountain tribe?" he called out.

"Of course I did!" Stul eased himself around in the saddle and looked back. "Why would you doubt it?"

"Because they stole our pack horses and all our belongings."

"Did you not see the awe in their eyes when they learned who I was?"

"No," Kuda's lips twisted into a sneer. "I saw them take whatever they wanted, though."

"Listen," Stul dragged his mount to a halt. "The fact that we are alive, unharmed and able to continue our journey on our ponies is testament enough to my reputation amongst the hill tribes."

"If you say so," Kuda grunted, sounding unconvinced.

"And another thing," Stul's face broke into a gloating grin. "They gave me some valuable information. They told me where the star-stone fell."

"Where?"

"The valley just beyond this ridge." Stul nodded toward the lip of the escarpment that rose steeply above them.

TEARS OF THE GODS

The short warrior went on relentlessly with his boasting as they picked their way up the long, stony slope. To Kuda's relief, they eventually crested the rise where the bragging hillman pulled his mount to a halt. He pointed over a small valley to a height crowned with a grey fortress. Its round tower sat behind an outer wall, which was lined by a cluster of huts just outside its sturdy gates. "Welcome to the home of my people. The Blue Mountain tribe!" he announced, while making a sweeping gesture which encompassed the whole valley.

As they drew nearer to the fortress Kuda roused himself and straightened in the saddle when he saw by the walls a row of six wooden crosses with human bodies nailed to them. A group of men, dressed in jackets of wolfskin and leggings of coarse cloth had gathered around the gates and were now sullenly watching their approach. Without pausing, Stul trotted past the group and through the open portals, where the clop of the ponies' hooves echoed off the rough walls surrounding the courtyard. Kuda looked around him as they dismounted. Inside the battlements, in addition to the round keep, there were barracks, animal pens, storehouses and armories. A burly figure with a bristling black beard appeared at the top of a short flight of steps that led up to the entrance to the keep. The man, wide in the shoulder and big in the gut stared stonily down at the new arrivals.

Stul approached him with his customary swagger announcing, "Greetings, Herger. I have returned!"

The man seemed to wince. "We thought you were dead," he muttered, sounding crestfallen.

"I was captured by the Khan's men, but they could not hold me," Stul replied, raising his voice as though he were addressing everyone within the fortress. "I fought my way to freedom over a carpet of their dead."

Herger sighed heavily and nodded toward Kuda. "Who is this?" he asked.

"An outlander I helped escape from slavery. After I ..."

Herger raised a hand to silence him. "He cannot stay. We do not need another mouth to feed."

"You might have need of my blade soon enough though," Kuda spoke up. "The Khan has commanded his divisions to scour these mountains for the star-stone and I doubt they will allow this fortress to impede them."

Herger's eyes stabbed at Kuda. "We do not fear the Kuruk," he snapped before turning back into the keep, motioning for them to follow.

There was a large hall beyond the door where several long tables were littered with the remains of a meal. A hush fell over the groups of men who were seated there as wolfish, bearded faces turned to survey the newcomers. A low muttering ensued when they recognized Stul.

"They don't seem very pleased to see you," Kuda murmured under his breath.

"Ha! Already they are jealous of my exploits, and I have not yet begun to regale them with my adventures," his short companion boomed.

A few of the men rose to leave, but Herger, obviously not wanting to suffer alone, waved them back into their seats with an angry gesture. Indicating a bench where the pair could sit, he dropped resignedly into a chair at the head of the table. Women with shapeless figures appeared from nowhere to shove wooden platters of grey meat and leather jacks of ale under the new arrival's noses.

Stul, attempting to talk and eat at the same time, began spraying the table top with half chewed meat. "I slew an entire troop of Kuruk in the foothills and ..."

One of the hillmen made a rude noise, interrupting the little man's flow. Herger saw his chance and spoke up quickly. "We do not fear the Khan's riders, for we have already retrieved the stone. It sits in this keep. When they arrive in this valley, we shall turn aside their wrath by presenting them with the accursed rock they seek." White teeth gleaming within his black beard, Herger went on. "There will be no battle but, barbarian, you may stay until the danger has passed. As you say, one more blade on the walls would not go amiss." The tribal leader abruptly stopped speaking to give all his attention to his food, thus making a point of not extending his invitation to Stul. A calculated insult.

In a burst of anger Stul surged to his feet. "I am a warrior of the Blue Mountain and have every right to be here," he yelled in a voice shrill with outrage.

Herger regarded him bleakly, then, with a malicious smile, said, "That is not disputed. Perhaps you can serve as our envoy to the Kuruk as you seem to have spent so much time in their company."

Gales of laughter greeted this remark. Stul, crimson faced, threw his wooden platter across the room and stamped out of the hall, an action which delighted the jeering tribesmen.

†

Crouching in the shadows, Kuda gazed up at the looming mass of the keep. He flashed a grin into the gloom when he saw how poorly constructed the walls were. The wide gaps between the rough-hewn blocks would provide him with hand and foot holds aplenty. Reaching up, he took his first handhold and heaved his body up off the ground. Naked but for a twist of cloth about his loins, he was confident that his lampblack smeared body would not be visible to any casual glance from the ground. Over one shoulder, he carried a leather satchel, empty but for a small dagger. He had left his weapons behind, knowing that the clink of metal against stone was the one sound that would alert even the sleepiest of guards. Hand over hand, he swiftly hauled himself upward in a smooth rhythm, his fingers and toes finding easy purchase. Soon, his questing fingers closed over the broad sill of the open window he had been aiming for. With one sudden explosive effort, he was through the window and dropping softly into the keep. He waited a moment, heart beating lightly as his senses strained to detect any sign of movement. All was still and quiet.

He was on a stone stairway that curved away both above and below him. The enclosed flight of stairs was lit only by the light of the flaming, pitch-soaked torches that stood in iron brackets along the walls. Silent as drifting smoke, Kuda ascended the staircase.

Finding himself in a hallway, the barbarian paused, his eyes level with the stone flagged floor. At the far end of the hallway, through an open archway, the stairs continued on upwards. Midway along the hallway, a door stood ajar and a brighter light burned within. Kuda felt a tremor of anxiety ripple down his spine. If he were discovered here there would be no explaining away his presence. He would assuredly join those unfortunates nailed to the crosses outside the gates. A lingering death. He reached into his satchel, took out the dagger and stole forward toward the door. He was perhaps six feet from the portal when he heard a snort, followed by the sound of heavy snoring from the room beyond. Kuda froze mid step, straining his ears for sounds of movement before padding forward to peer into the room. The chamber was filled with a large bed, on which were sprawled three sleeping figures: two naked women and a rotund hairy Herger. The chieftain lay on his back, snoring loudly. To Kuda's relief, the noise did not seem to disturb the women, who slept on peacefully. They were probably well used to the racket, he reflected, backing away.

Resuming his ascent, Kuda climbed the next flight of stairs, which ended at a single, iron-bound door. He eyed the stout barrier dubiously. If the door was locked then he was undone. Any attempt by him to batter it down would rouse the whole keep. Bracing himself, he lifted the iron latch. The door edged open with a slight creak and a waft of stale air emanated from the dark space beyond. Thrusting the door aside, he burst into the chamber.

Slowly, he lowered his knife and straightened up from the fighting crouch he had dropped into. Releasing his breath, he thanked whatever Gods were smiling down upon him. The chamber was deserted. Reaching back beyond the door, he lifted a torch from its bracket and raised it up.

The wavering glow of the torch revealed a small, round, windowless room stacked with a collection of weapons and a few locked, wooden chests. Sitting on the floor in the center of the room, looking strangely out of place, was a rock the size of a man's head. Moving swiftly into the chamber, his feet slowed until he stopped to stand gaping down at the boulder. He saw only a nondescript dark rock with some lighter striations interrupting its coarse surface. It looked battered, as though it had indeed been scoured by great forces during a headlong journey at incredible velocities through the shadowed gulfs of space. Unremarkable looking though it was, an unnatural tightness in his gut and a shortening of his breath told him that, without any doubt, he was looking at a tear of the God's.

†

The hulking barbarian dropped softly into the shadows at the base of the keep. Hefting the satchel onto his shoulder, heavy now with the star-stone it contained, he moved off at a crouch across the darkened courtyard. Keeping to the darkness, he stopped when he reached the foot of a flight of steps that led up to a bastion jutting out from the fortress walls. After a brief pause to listen intently for any sign that he had been spotted he began climbing the stairs. Approaching the top step, he slowly raised his head to peer over it. In the glow of a dying brazier, he saw a sentry in a wolfskin cap asleep on his spear. Flicking his eyes left and right along the battlements he saw no-one else. The safest course of action would be to slit the guard's throat. He raised the knife in his hand, but remained on the step. Lips compressed into a thin line, he fought an inner battle. Cold blooded murder after breaking bread with the hillmen did not sit right with him. Slipping the knife back into his satchel, he stole up the final few steps as silently as a cat. A few seconds later, he was on the bastion's flat top, melting into the shadow of a huge wooden catapult that was sited there. Crossing to a pile of boulders that were placed close by as ammunition for the catapult, he began groping about in the dark until his searching fingers closed on the pack he had stashed there earlier. Dragging the bundle from its hiding place, he removed and hastily donned the thick clothes it contained, along with his saber and a vest of chain mail. Crossing over to the wall, he pulled himself up onto the battlements and looked down. The walls of the fortress were twenty feet high, and though thick enough to withstand siege engines were as poorly constructed as the keep. Again, there would be handholds aplenty. Even in the gloom, his descent to the ground outside would only take seconds. Pausing to make sure that the star-stone was secure in his satchel, he swung one leg out over the coping and froze in that position. Slowly and with infinite care, he drew his leg back up. His keen eyes had detected movement out in the valley. Drawing back into the shadows of the battlements, he strained his eyes into the outer darkness. Somewhere out there, men and beasts were moving, lots of them. The Northman pricked his ears until the clink of hooves and the creaking of saddles came to him on the cold wind. The Kuruk had arrived and were spreading, unnoticed, across the valley floor like an army of wraiths.

Wheeling away from the parapet his eyes darted about the bastion. He let out a string of oaths, cursing the ill-luck that had dogged him ever since he had set foot in this benighted land. Now he was trapped between the Khan's riders and the hillmen. His mind whirled. He did not have time to return the stone to the keep. At any second now, the alarm would be raised and the fortress would be alive with enraged tribesmen. Cursing all the Gods, he slipped the satchel from his shoulder.

SEVEN

They rode in a solid mass that clogged the floor of the valley. The Khan's killers, veterans of a hundred battles, men forged and tempered in the furnace of war, razor-sharp and resilient as the finest steel. The first rays of the sun slanted in across the crests of the mountains and lit their unsheathed blades into a thousand dazzles. Shielding his eyes, Kuda turned away from the sight to look down the line of the fortress wall to where Herger stood silently with a group of his hetmen. The spectacle of the army ranged against them had stilled their howling tongues and they looked on in awe and apprehension at the array of armored horsemen sprawling across the landscape.

Stroking his beard, Herger continued to stare at the riders a moment longer before turning to his lieutenants. "They are not here to destroy us," he proclaimed in a strong voice. "They are here for the star-stone. And we shall deliver it to them without delay." Swinging away, he descended the staircase from the battlements with the anxious-looking group trailing behind him.

Turning to gaze back out over the wall, Kuda watched as the Khan's warriors slid from their unkempt ponies. Each man had a large shield strapped to his back and a gleaming blade grasped in his fist. A medley of sounds came to his ears: shouted commands, ribald laughter, the scraping of sharpening stones on blades and the neighing of many horses. They seemed impatient and arrogant enough to attempt to take the fortress without waiting for any parley with its occupants.

Stul appeared at his elbow, sleepy eyes widening in astonishment at the sight before him. "The Khan has sent an army to recapture me," he spluttered.

184

Kuda snorted in derision. "Don't flatter yourself, little man. They know only that a tear of the Gods fell into this valley and that this fortress stands in their way."

"Then we must give it to them, and quickly," he cried out in a voice close to hysteria.

Kuda smiled thinly.

✝

As Uracc ran his eyes over the people standing upon the fortress walls, they abruptly stopped at a figure standing head and shoulders above the others. When he recognized the giant standing upon the battlements, hatred flared hotly through his guts. Here, at last, was the outlander bastard who had shamed him in front of his Father. The barbarian seemed to sense the force of his hatred for he abruptly turned away and disappeared from sight below the embrasures. Uracc allowed himself a smile, his teeth brilliant against the smoky yellow of his skin. The outlander was trapped within the Blue Mountain fortress. It was fortunate indeed that the trail he and his men had been following had led them here in time to join the assault. All around him, the Kuruk warriors were preparing for war; tightening the straps on their lacquered breastplates and thumbing the edges of their curved swords. Others pulled on their fur trimmed helmets and fastened the buckles beneath their chins. The ponies were being gathered together and led to the rear. Today, they would be fighting on foot. The small army's advance into the mountains had left a bloody trail of maimed and tortured bodies. Vigorous questioning of the locals had left the raiders in no doubt that the star-stone they sought was behind the fortress walls.

✝

The occupants of the fortress watched the enemy's preparations with trepidation. None of the pragmatic mountain people really believed that the presentation of a worthless rock, even one that had fallen from the sky, would turn aside the Kuruks' attack. Arming themselves, they took up their stations on the parapets behind the fort's closed and barred gates. Some of the shaggily dressed men even whirled slingshots around their heads and let fly.

A raw wind was lifting small spirals of powdered snow, sending them spinning across the rocky ground in front of the fortress as, recurved bows strung and held ready, full quivers bouncing at their hips a screen of Kuruk archers advanced from the main group. They strode confidently to take up positions amongst the straggle of mud-walled huts outside the walls. There they waited with nocked arrows, holding their fire until the main assault force assembled behind them.

From his vantage point upon the bastion, Kuda studied the gathering force with puzzlement. The warriors, under the direction of their Orkhons, were forming up in column. They had sheathed their weapons and made no effort to construct the scaling ladders, which they would surely need to storm the walls. The big flat shields each man carried also remained firmly strapped to their backs, where they would be of little use.

A roar of rage rose from the keep behind him. Kuda spun about.

Herger and his retinue erupted from the tower's doorway, weapons raised. Frothing at the mouth, the Blue Mountain tribe's leader paused to glare around him until his eyes fixed on Kuda.Lips twisting angrily, he pointed a condemning, damning finger at the outlander. "You," he hissed.

✝

TEARS OF THE GODS

An Orkhon took several paces forward before he stopped and tugged out his saber. Chest expanding beneath his lacquered breastplate, he drew a breath and bellowed an order. At his command, the column stirred. Breath steaming in the cold air, the warriors began trudging silently towards the fortress, all the time maintaining their tight formation.

A couple of hillmen barged past Kuda to begin preparing the nearby catapult for firing. The machine's firing arm began to creak and move as the men threw themselves upon the windlass which drew it back down into the firing position. A quick look told Kuda that Herger was leading a band of his furious hetmen across the courtyard, directly toward the bastion. An arrow zipped in over the parapet to thud into the back of one of the windlass operators. He fell, face first, his legs twitching violently. His startled partner almost let go of the wooden wheel. Cursing, Kuda leapt to the spokes and began heaving upon the handles. The arm lowered quickly and the remaining operator engaged the lever that secured the firing arm against the tension of the massive crossbow.

The two men grinned at each other before Kuda stooped to the pile of nearby ammunition to pluck a rock from the pile. He thrust it at the man. "Here, load this and fire the damned thing," he grunted.

Taking the heavy rock, the man rolled it into the catapult's waiting bowl and turned away, saying, "I must wait for the order." They ducked as another arrow rattled the embrasures.

"Order! What order? The enemy are almost at the walls!" Kuda roared.

"Herger must give the command to fire," the man snapped back. "Look, here he comes now."

Kuda looked up to see Herger and his bristling pack leaping up the bastion steps.

"So I see," he said before pushing the catapult operator aside and knocking back the handle that held the ratchet. With a great crack, the firing arm whipped forward to shoot the rock high into the air. Kuda's eyes followed the flight of the stone until it landed harmlessly, well away from any of the enemy.

"A wasted shot!" the operator clawed at his beard. "We did not sight the catapult, you Northern idiot!"

Kuda's meaty fist hammered into the man's jaw, sending him sprawling onto the flagstones. "Don't worry about it," he snarled.

Heaving a rock from the pile of catapult ammunition, Kuda rushed over to the head of the steps and hoisted it over his head. Herger, puffing and panting at the head of his mob of howling hetmen, looked up and saw what Kuda was about to do. He threw himself flat. The barbarian hurled the heavy boulder down the steps. The projectile missed the prone Herger by a whisker and plunged on to pulverize the chest of the man behind him. That man cartwheeled down the steps to carry two more men away in his helpless tumble. The narrow stone stairway became a tangle of sprawling, cursing tribesmen. Roaring oaths, Herger lurched back to his feet. Without hesitation, Kuda sprang down the steps and kicked the chieftain in the face. The impact sent Herger tumbling down the stairs, where his considerable bulk added to the confusion.

Jumping back, the Northman raced across the bastion to where he had earlier secured a length of rope to an embrasure. Plucking up the thick coils, he glanced over the parapet. The sun chose that moment to burst out over the mountain tops, lighting the valley with dramatic color and brilliance. The attackers had reached the foot of the wall. Frowning in puzzlement, Kuda watched as the first eight ranks of the compact column threw themselves down onto all fours. In that position, with the large shields strapped to their backs, they formed a platform onto which scrambled the next four ranks, who also quickly got down on hands and knees. The sequence continued, until, in the blink of an eye, the warriors had formed a broad, human stairway that almost reached the top of the twenty-foot wall. Close upon their heels, the main column of warriors dashed forward. Without hesitation, they began to swarm upwards upon the backs of their comrades. Above them, any defender foolish enough to raise his head above the parapet became a pincushion.

Shaking his head in astonishment, Kuda turned his attention back to the rope and threw it over the wall. This was the moment he had been waiting for, the moment the attackers and defenders were fully occupied. Clambering over the broad coping, he swiftly lowered himself down the rope and dropped the last few feet to the valley floor. Glancing around, he saw that the Kuruk, who had reached the top of the wall, were closing with the defenders. More attackers were surging up the human staircase to follow them. Amid the curses and grunts, the clash of metal and the cries of anger and pain, Kuda could see that the Khan's warriors were being badly mauled. Dozens of them were dying, their bodies flung back from the walls. Yet, they kept pressing forward, ignoring their losses, charge after charge, like waves pounding on a rocky foreshore. Then the defenders broke and the Kuruk were among them. Though the hillmen howled their defiance and threw themselves at the invaders with a manic rage, they could not prevent the Khan's ruthless, professional warriors from spreading out along the walls. For a moment, Kuda stood transfixed, watching the steppe-riders forcing the hillmen back, their gleaming blades rising and falling in sprays of gore. With a slight shake of his head, he brought his attention back to his own predicament. He had seen enough; the fortress was doomed. It was time to make haste. Judging the moment

189

right, he set off across the rocky terrain, keeping well clear of the fighting. When he had gained some distance, he paused and turned around to gauge his position in relation to the bastion he had just vacated. He could see hundreds of struggling men locked in a deadly fight along the line of the fortress walls. Ignoring the uproar of hoarse shouts and clashing steel, he quickly got his bearings and, altering direction slightly, headed off at a trot. A little further on, his eyes fixed upon the star-stone. It was exactly where he'd expected it to be when he had carefully marked its flight after launching it from the catapult. With a whoop of triumph, he retrieved it from the ground and placed it in his satchel. Firing the stone from the catapult had been risky, but it was the only way he could think of to unburden himself of the incriminating rock and get it safely out of the besieged fort. Well satisfied, he swung the heavy bag upon his shoulder as his eyes scoured the valley for the Kuruk horse lines. The boulder-strewn valley floor was open and exposed, and he soon spotted the ponies all gathered together in a small herd. He set off once again, picking his way carefully over the loose rocks.

He had not gone far when an arrow whizzed close past his head. So close, he felt the wind of its passing. Slamming to a halt, he whirled around, hand snatching at his saber. Kuruk warriors, three of them, were running furiously toward him, their red faces glaring under metal helmets. Boots scraped on rock behind him and he turned to see more warriors blocking his way. He was surrounded.

As they began to advance on him in unison Kuda recognized their leader. It was his old nemesis, the tall, well-built young man he had spared for the sake of his Father. Shaking his head ruefully, he spat on the ground. He recalled words he'd overheard often enough when listening to old warriors yarning about the campfire: "One good deed will kill you quicker than an arrow through the heart." How true that was.

Dropping the heavy satchel, he drew a long-bladed knife from his boot.

Uracc's face was set and unreadable, but his eyes were murderous. "I knew you would not stand and fight with your new friends," he snarled, his voice thick, strangled with emotion. "We were watching and waiting for you to run away, you treacherous Northern ape!"

Kuda's eyes stabbed at the young man. "Your Father is not here to save you this time whelp."

The youthful warrior threw back his head and howled like a madman. With death in his eye he leapt forward, swinging his sword like a butcher's cleaver. Kuda deflected the wild slashing cut and rammed his shoulder into the youth's chest, slamming him backwards into his charging companions. Spinning about, he met the rush of those behind him with singing steel. There was the moist impact of blade upon flesh. One of the attackers reeled back, blood spurting from his sword arm. A forward roll under slicing blades took Kuda out of the circle of his attackers. Without pausing, they surged after him in a howling wave. Springing to his feet, Kuda met their charge, shouting and lunging with the point to drive them back. With a strangled cry of pain, a warrior collapsed to the ground, hamstrung by a knife he never even glimpsed. Ducking under another wild slash, the barbarian's saber tip flickered out to open a throat. Jumping over the downed man, he fell amongst them, stabbing, cutting, and slicing.

The steppe-riders fell back, exchanging glances, visibly stunned by the ferocity of their supposed 'victim'. Where they had been expecting only a token resistance, they now found themselves desperately fighting for their lives. A civilized man in Kuda's situation would have accepted the inevitability of his death at their hands. The sobering realization that they were not facing a civilized man, one they could easily murder, abruptly dawned on them. This was a formidable warrior who opposed them. A ferocious killer from the wastelands of the North who fought with the strength of ten and whose people seemingly had no word for 'surrender'. Uncertain now, they stood huddled, shoulder to shoulder, panting hard and staring. With the bloodlust of battle contorting his features, Kuda cut a ferocious and terrifying figure.

The fires of hate smoldering in Uracc's eyes flared brighter when he saw his companion's hesitation. "Cowards!" he screamed and, full of the idiotic indestructible confidence of youth, he rushed alone at the giant barbarian, his saber a whirl of blurring steel. Once again, Kuda met the mad charge, keeping the youth at bay with a series of sweeps and thrusts. Frustrated, Uracc lunged his saber toward the outlander's chest. Kuda swayed back and at the same time scraped his blade up along the length of overextended steel. With a deft twist of wrist, he hooked the young man's sword out of his grasp. It went spinning through the air to clang upon the rocky ground. Dropping his own saber, Kuda reached out and grabbed the upper edge of Uracc's breastplate and yanked him closer. The young warrior's head jerked backward, exposing his throat. In that instant Kuda buried the broad blade of his knife into the soft flesh there. His blade sliced through the young man's windpipe and the great arteries of the neck to grate on the spine. The young man's eyes stared incredulously into Kuda's for a second or two before they rolled back white. Blood bursting brightly from his mouth, he swayed on his feet. His knees gave way under him and he crumpled and dropped like a felled tree.

There was a collective intake of breath from the bunched warriors. Kuda took a pace backwards, watching them warily. Silently, they all stared at one another for a moment before an archer strolled casually out from behind the group, an arrow already nocked to his bow. The Northman let out a slow, heavy sigh. The bowman continued walking until he was sure of a clear shot, then he raised the recurved bow, drawing the string back to its fullest extent. Kuda glared at the man until a foot of crimson-washed steel sprang from the archer's chest in a spray of blood and bone. The bowman fell sideways to the ground, releasing the arrow, which scythed deep into the grouped warriors, felling two more. Snatching up his saber, Kuda let out a bloodcurdling roar and bounded towards the startled group. They reeled apart and fled. They couldn't help themselves, the fear the barbarian aroused was primal. Kuda did not pursue them. His feet slowed and he came to a halt, panting mightily.

Stul paused to free his blade from deep in the bowman's lungs before joining Kuda.

The Northman grinned. "I never thought I'd be happy to see you again, you back-stabbing little toad."

"First, I led you to the star-stone and now, I have saved your life," the short man sniffed, ramming his sword back into its scabbard. "Yet you still fail to appreciate my heroic efforts."

Sheathing his own weapons, Kuda clapped a big hand on Stul's shoulder. "You are wrong. I do appreciate your talents, and, if I ever want anyone else stabbing in the back, you will be the first person I call upon."Raising his eyes, the giant barbarian looked back toward the fortress, which was now burning. "What about your loyalty to your tribe?"

"Bah!" Stul dismissed the question with a snort. "They insulted me. Why should I fight for them? Herger was a fool, he should have fled while he had the chance."

Kuda nodded. "If he's still alive, he'll be telling the Kuruk all about me and the star-stone, so we don't have much time."

"You have it?"

Kuda retrieved the satchel. "Right here. Now, let's see if you are as good a horse-thief as you are a backstabber."

†

When the smell of manure became overpowering, they knew they were close to the horse lines. Keeping low, the pair edged up to a large boulder. They could now hear the impatient stamping of hooves, the occasional vibrating fart of a pony breaking wind and the soothing sounds made by unseen steppe-riders, who were whistling between their teeth or murmuring soft nonsense as they attended to their charges. Peering around the rocky outcrop, Kuda could see picket ropes, thick with tethered animals. A sudden uproar from the direction of the fortress caused Kuda's head to jerk around. Roaring mightily, masses of Kuruk poured in through the gates, which had been thrown open. The distracted horse guards crowded together to witness the last stages of the battle. Kuda motioned Stul forward, confident they would not be heard above the attackers' shouts of triumph, and the cries for mercy and despair from the defenders. Kuda knew there would be no mercy this day. The steppe-riders had suffered in the mountains and needed to satisfy their bloodlust.

Circling around the rocks, the pair stealthily approached the nearest ponies. While Kuda stroked their noses to prevent any nervous whickering, Stul untied two of the beasts. Together, they led them away. Kuda looked over his shoulder, checking the excited guards. All their attention was fixed upon the battle. Satisfied they had not been noticed, he padded over to a pile of saddle bridles and blankets and helped himself. Stul did likewise. Soon they were mounted and picking their way unhurriedly up the rugged slope on two shaggy-maned mares. At the crest of the rise, they paused a moment, hearts beating swiftly as their senses strained to detect any sign of pursuit. There was none. Below them, the fortress of the Blue Mountain tribe burned beneath a pillar of thick, black smoke. The battle had fizzled out, but a few desultory cries of anguish amidst the crackle and pop of the burning stronghold could still be heard. Through the drifts of smoke, Kuda saw gangs of steppe-riders rounding up the defeated mountain people, and searching for loot and booty. He cursed when he recognized the unmistakable bulk of Herger amongst the survivors.

EIGHT

Laying on his belly in the long grass, Kuda screwed up his eyes against the glare of the setting sun, and ran them along the crater's saw-edged crest. The Kuruk hordes may have left their winter camp, but the Khan's personal guard and all his retinue surely remained. Those elite troops would have posted sentries on the heights.

Stul shifted uncomfortably beside him. "What are we waiting for? You have the stone, so let us present it to the Khan and claim my rich reward and your slave girl. Why are we crawling around in the dirt like beetles?"

"You don't think the Khan's guards would also crave a rich reward?" Kuda answered, without looking at the shorter man, who lay beside him. "If we simply walked up to them with the rock, they would cut our throats and claim any reward for themselves."

Stul sighed heavily. "So, what do we do?"

"We wait until dark, then …" Kuda stopped mid-sentence when the ground trembled beneath him. A shrieking roar struck them like a physical force, like a storm-driven wave. It stunned their ear drums and startled their senses. A great column of bright, orange flame erupted from the base of the crater. If the two men had not been lying flat, they would have been blown off their feet with the force of it.

Stul began screaming. "The dragon awakens!"

The great flame lit the grasslands like noonday. Smoke blew in a screaming cloud across the sky. Then, as abruptly as it had started, it stopped, the thunder of it rolling away across the plain.

"I told you! I told you!" Stul shrieked on hysterically. "Now you have seen it. Dragonfire from the caves beneath the Ziggurat, where the dragon dwells!"

With an effort, Kuda managed to shrug off the icy wind of dread that blew across his skin. "Still your tongue, numbskull!" he hissed in the panicking man's ear. "Let's get back to the horses now. Stay low, for I have seen lookouts on the ridges above us."

✝

The hobbled mares were waiting where they had left them, in a slight depression and out of sight of any watchers on the crater's rim. Kuda unhooked the heavy satchel, which contained the star-stone, from his saddle horn. "It will be dark soon. We can use that cave beneath the escarpment to enter the crater."

Stul looked at him, jaws agape. "Enter a dragon's lair? Are you mad?" His blood chilled at the very thought.

"You can wait here with the horses. If I do not return by morning, then leave."

"Why should I wait?" Stul snarled suddenly. "To be devoured by the dragon? To be flayed alive by the Khan's mountain troops, who cannot be more than a day behind us? Where is the profit? If you are successful, all you will carry away with you is a slave girl. Pah! You …"

Kuda backhanded him across the face. The force of it sent Stul over backwards. Kuda stood over him. The small wiry man was trying to crawl away from the brutal, scarred face and what he saw in it, but the thick grass prevented his retreat.

"You will stay," Kuda growled. "Because I need these mounts, and if they are not here when I return, then I will track you down, hamstring you and leave you out there for the wolves. My oath on it."

Without another word, Kuda shrugged the satchel onto his shoulder and stalked off into the gathering darkness. Stul stared after him, his split lips twisting into a gloating little smile.

✝

In places, the grass was still smoldering. In the flickering light of the small fires, Kuda could make out the long tongue of scorched earth, which marked the dragon's lair. With the sheer face of the escarpment looming over him against the newly born stars, he slowly and cautiously approached the huge cave opening. Stepping into the dark maw, he stretched out a hand to steady himself. His fingers came away greasy and thick with ash. He stopped dead, staring ahead into impenetrable blackness. "Dragon." The word ghosted out from him. With great effort, he pulled himself back from the dark imaginings of his own mind and reached over his shoulder to loosen his saber in its scabbard. His jaw tightened as he strode forward. Esmira was waiting.

✝

"Haven't you finished yet?" Esmira asked irritably.

"Not quite, my child," Salima, the old woman-servant, answered. "Have patience, it is almost done."

Esmira frowned and sighed theatrically. It seemed like hours since she'd been called into the Khan's presence. She was sitting in her yurt being prepared by her attendants for her ascent to the Ziggurat. There, she would stand at the Khan's side to witness the awakening of the dragon. It was an event so significant and momentous that she felt tense and on edge. She had been told that the dragon's keeper had somehow sensed the presence of the final star-stone. It was close by, apparently. Close enough to begin the ceremonies. Her eyes flitted restlessly about the tent's interior. Sheepskin rugs were scattered over the earth floor. A fire burned in a heavy iron brazier, for it was dark now and there was a chill in the air.

"Now, stand up and let's look at you," Salima said, stepping back.

There was an intake of breath and murmurs of admiration from the gathered women as Esmira got to her feet.

She stretched like a cat before walking across the floor to study herself in a long, ebony-framed mirror. She was dressed in a light, almost sheer, cotton gown dyed a pale indigo blue. Her waist was cinched by a glittering belt, her breasts jutted boldly against the thin cotton. With the light from the brazier behind her, it looked as if her naked body were wreathed in a dawn mist. Round her neck were three bands of beaten gold chain and about her temples was a circlet studded with precious stones. She tilted back her head and arched her neck. Shining midnight tresses danced across her shoulders as she raised her arms and pirouetted once, twice, and then a third time. The dress billowed out and swirled round her. It was so fine, she could barely feel it. She might have been clothed in air. In the glass, the gold and precious stones sparkled and glittered.

Esmira laughed. "Am I ready?" she asked teasingly.

"You are not only ready, child," Salima answered softly. "You are beautiful. A fitting bride for the Kha Khan."

Salima's eyes were moist. Behind her, the other women cupped their hands and applauded. Several were crying, too.

"Then, shall we go?" Esmira asked.

Salima nodded and took her hand.

†

A detachment of the Khan's bodyguards were waiting for them at the foot of the Ziggurat's stairs. As Esmira mounted the first steps, she heard music and glanced up. The layered terraces of the pyramidal structure were lit with blazing tapers and filled with the Khan's musicians. At her appearance, they began to play. The fluting of pipes and the beat of goatskin drums lifted into the air and seemed to hang like a canopy over her. Esmira smiled, waved and regally ascended.

✝

Taking each step quietly and straining his ears, Kuda crept forward. His eyes tried to find something to focus on but there was nothing in front of him except pitch blackness. Blackness and a smell so foul and strange, it seemed to cover him like a layer of soot. It must be the smell of the dragon, he reasoned, for nothing in the known world smelled like that. Beneath his hands, the surrounding rock walls were warm to the touch. Just then, a small light appeared in the distance, glowing cherry red. As he progressed, it was joined by others, all of them pulsating. In their dim radiance, he made out the shape of the tunnel ahead. It was becoming uncomfortably hot. As he closed upon the pulsating lights, Kuda realized they were actually rocks that had been fired to a red heat. Brushing the sweat from his face, he kept moving. Ahead of him, the residual heat shimmer rendered the cracked tunnel's interior trembling and indistinct as it receded into the distance. This was no place to linger. If the dragon breathed again, he would be incinerated. Pressing doggedly on, he discerned another solid glow emanating from the gloom. Increasing his pace, he stumbled to the tunnel's end to find himself staring out over a broad sweep of cracked and fire-scarred paving. The paving formed the floor of a vast chamber, an empty space bathed in a harsh, unwelcoming white light.

With the air around him becoming almost too hot to breathe, he stole forward and out into the open.

Proceeding warily across the cavernous space, he tipped a glance upward. All around him, great walls of ancient stone reared aloft to dizzying heights. Turning slowly in a circle, his mind struggled with the realization of where he was; he was now deep within the innermost structure of the Ziggurat itself. He was also far beneath the earth, which meant that only the pyramid's apex was visible above the ground. Like an iceberg, two thirds of the mammoth structure remained forever hidden beneath the surface. That was not all. He stopped short when he saw what was contained within the pyramid. Before him, a tower of gleaming metal lanced upwards. It was straight as a spear and made from some hammered, bright alloy he did not recognize. It was held upright inside a complex assembly of iron struts that forked away from each other at right angles. The tower's base, wreathed in steam and smoke, was held above the chamber's floor by this framework. He moved closer until he was almost beneath the tower. Enormous, bell-shaped nozzles hung overhead, and the cradle supporting the tower enclosed him in a thicket of iron struts. His senses reeled, he had never seen anything like it before, let alone imagined anything like it. His mind held no frame of reference for what his eyes were revealing to him. Not sure whether he was dreaming or going insane, he shook his head, coughed and spat. The dragon reek was now overpowering. Despite this, he still stubbornly refused to believe in the existence of such a beast. The foul air was oppressive, thick and so full of strange menace,that his wilderness-bred instincts were screaming at him to keep moving. The only way forward was upward. So, pulling the scabbard tighter on his back, he crossed to the foot of the tower's iron framework. Reaching out, he scorched his flesh as he grabbed hold of the hot metal. Ignoring the pain, he began the climb.

✝

As Esmira neared the apex of the Ziggurat, she lifted her chin to see the Kha Khan standing there, waiting for her. A tremulous half smile spread across her lovely, tilting lips as she raised her eyes to meet the Khan's stare. His black eyes sparkled with pleasure out of a face that was suggestive of great strength of will. His chin jutted, his mouth was flat and hard, his forehead low and thoughtful. Hero to his people, he stood tall, attired in the full panoply of war, armed and armored, resplendent in a long coat of mail polished so brightly, it shone like silver. The sword at his hip, a heavy blade, was scabbarded in soft leather trimmed with gold and his blue cloak was lined with the fur of a snow leopard.

She locked her eyes with his, almost daring him to deny her beauty. He was undoubtedly a savage, but during the weeks and months she had been the Khan's concubine, his allure had grown. With a mixture of consternation and pleasure, she recalled the night he had first summoned her to his bed. She had led a sheltered life and had never been naked in the presence of a man before. When he had reached out for her she had stiffened, her instincts telling her to reject him. But, even though her brain was a vortex of emotions, thoughts, memories and apprehension, she had forced herself to relax. Before she was consciously aware of it she had allowed him to stroke and kiss her until she was hungry for some form of relief from the unbearable sexual tension that was gripping her. His hard body descended upon her, causing a succession of dizzying sensations, each more exquisite than the last, each threatening more and more to drive her over a precipice at which she might otherwise have baulked, until she was plunging through space into the abyss of total sexual fulfillment. The wanton memories caused her gaze to grow hot. The Khan leered down at her as booming brass gongs shivered the night air.

✝

Hand over hand, Kuda ascended the iron assembly. Although there were handholds aplenty, it was a long, hard climb, with the strap of the heavy leather bag containing the star-stone digging into his shoulder. His mail shirt, coupled with the long saber strapped to his back, also weighed heavily. Sweat ran freely into his eyes and he felt his fingers slipping by tiny fractions each time he grasped a beam. To one side, the gleaming wall of the strange tower kept him company. Devoid of any features, the wall scrolled slowly by, uniformly smooth and snow-white in the unrelenting white glare. Jamming his boots in at whatever twisted angle he could manage, he paused. Then, gripping with both hands, he leaned outwards, craning his neck to chance a glance upwards. He gave a grunt of satisfaction; not far now. Gritting his teeth, he began to clamber ever higher. A few minutes later, he got a grip with both hands, heaved himself up onto the final beam to chest level, then hauled the rest of his body wearily after.

Balanced precariously on a narrow strip of iron and conscious of the fatal drop on either side of him, he cast his eyes around. He was now level with the tower's cone-shaped top, which was, in turn, completely overshadowed by walls of heavy masonry. He could see a doorway opening into the tower top. The metal walkway leading to it extended from an open archway in the pyramid wall. The archway was the only exit and the only way to reach it was from a ledge that ran around the interior walls. There was a final, treacherous five-foot gap between the beam and that ledge. Kuda set his jaw. Breathing deeply and regularly, he slowly rose to his feet to face the gap. Arms outstretched for balance, he advanced by inches until he stood at the farthest extension of the beam. Staring straight ahead, he saw that the ledge beyond the gap was narrow and devoid of any handholds.

With a weary sigh, Kuda hitched up the heavy star-stone satchel to a more secure position and backed up a few, careful paces. Taking fast, cat-like steps, he plunged forward and leapt. There was an instant of flight before he hit the stonework and bounced off. Scrabbling frantically for purchase, he managed to hang on, arresting his backward slide into the void. Muttering thanks to whichever God might be listening, he clung there, suspended precariously over the drop, gasping for breath. When he had sufficiently recovered, he heaved himself up onto the crumbling ledge. With his back pressed against the stone wall, he worked his way gingerly along until he was positioned over the archway. Squatting down, he hooked his fingers onto the arches lintel and swung out and round to land on the threshold of the opening. Rising on shaky legs, he looked around. A long, tunnel-like passage stretched away before him. Turning, he glanced back across the metal walkway toward the open door that led into the tower. The space beyond that hatch-like opening was filled with a faint iridescent glow, quite unlike anything Kuda had ever seen before. As he stood pondering the strange luminescence, a quiet susurration came to his ears, as if the chamber were whispering to itself. All around him he suddenly sensed the presence of some alien malevolence. Muttering darkly, he pivoted on his heel and darted off down the bare stone passageway.

✝

TEARS OF THE GODS

Esmira stood proudly, her head high, her gaze sweeping over the throng of people assembled about the Ziggurat. Hair shining rich and dark as jet, brown eyes glinting with triumph, she glanced sidelong at the impressive figure of the Great Khan who stood beside her. She noticed his expression was grave. Although she felt she was about to burst with joy, she composed her own features to match his. Once more, she stared out over the crowd. A heavy silence descended as the musicians stopped playing and, for the first time, she noticed a peculiar stillness over the gathering. A pall of fear hung over them. She licked her lips and swallowed, the somber atmosphere finally reminding her of the purpose of this occasion: to witness the awakening of a dragon.

†

Kuda took a fresh grip on his fear and slowed his pace as darkness closed about him. He crept forward as swiftly and silently as he could, until he came to a flight of broad and shallow steps, worn wax smooth and uneven with age. He took them two at a time, knife in hand for anyone he might meet at the top. At the top of the flight, the light increased as he emerged into a round chamber. From its size and shape, he surmised that he was now inside the strange looking temple that sat atop the Ziggurat. In the half-light, he peered around at the worn-down flagstones and slim pillars holding up a sagging roof. There was a stone altar in the shadows with a weirdly carved stone screen behind it. There were no furnishings or fabrics, just an air of neglect over everything, a temple without Gods or worshippers, in name only.

†

Stul edged to the front of the crowd to stand like everyone else, gazing up in wonder and awe at the splendid figure of the Kha Khan and his beautiful new wife. Gaining entry to the crater had turned out to be easy. The lookouts and perimeter guards had abandoned their posts to join the gathering throng, not wanting to miss out on such a momentous occasion. So much for Kuda's stealthy approach, he smirked and then winced. His face still hurt where the barbarian's heavy hand had struck him. With a tight smile, he thought of how he had already paid the outlander back for that blow. A ripple of alarm suddenly washed through the people around him. There were gasps of surprise as the Khan's elite guard raced up the Ziggurat's steps.

✝

The crowd were staring, pale-faced and shocked, at something behind her. Esmira turned around. The joy in her eyes died and she paled. Uncertainly, her hand lifted to her throat and she made a small choking sound.

The Khan also turned took a half-step forward and stared, frowning, at the barbarian, who rose up from the temple's doorway like something summoned from some dark corner of hell. Clothed in heavy mail and leather, his hair filthy and matted, his savage features streaked with soot and grime, Kuda paced into the torchlight.

The Khan's face darkened with anger. "How … what are you doing here? You dare to …"

"I have the final tear of the Gods here in this bag," Kuda interrupted impatiently, holding up the leather satchel.

The Khan's eyes darted to the heavy bag then back to Kuda's face. He nodded slowly. "The keeper told me that the star-stone would arrive tonight, but he never explained the manner of its conveyance. If what you say is true, barbarian, then you have done me a great service. You shall be rewarded."

"The girl," Kuda rumbled, nodding toward Esmira. "I want the girl. Free her and the stone is yours."

At first, the Khan looked astonished at Kuda's request, then he barked a laugh. "Is that all? I could give you a thousand women and a palace full of gold to enjoy them in."

"Just the girl," Kuda repeated, keeping his gaze nailed to the Khan's eyes.

There was a long silence before the Khan laughed again. It started as a splutter of startled disbelief, before becoming loud and genuine. Kuda watched him impassively. Finally, the Khan's laughter slowed to a halt. He cleared his throat and shook his head, a man apparently bemused by what was before him.

Esmira turned, her face pale and set. In a small voice, she said, "I will not go to him."

Ignoring her, the Khan leaned forward, eyes still locked with Kuda's. His tone hardened. "Show me the stone."

Kuda unslung the satchel and tipped the stone out so that it landed at his feet.

They all stared at an unremarkable steppe rock, covered in lichen and dirt.

"You arrogant outlander scum!" the Khan shrieked in a voice filled with shock and outrage. "Do you seek to mock me?" His sword leapt into his hand.

By his side, Esmira regarded the grimy intruder disdainfully. "He is a moonstruck lunatic, my lord. I knew it from the first moment I saw him."

Kuda glared down at the rock that was so similar to a million others lying out on the steppe yet so different from the one he had stolen from the Blue Mountain tribe.

"Stul!" He spat the name, a red mist forming at the corners of his vision. He felt the upwelling urge to kill something, hot and instant, there in his guts, muscles and limbs.

The Khan's personal guard, murderous looking ruffians, clattered to a skidding halt around their Kha Khan .

An unholy mad spark ignited in the Khan's eyes. Once again, his voice rose almost to a shriek. "Treachery! I am surrounded by plotters seeking to rob me of my promised destiny. You!" He hissed the word at Esmira, rounding on her fiercely, his voice rising to a pitch of hysteria. "You arrived with this arrogant foreign thug. You are in league with him. You conspire together to prevent the rising of the dragon. Why else would he attempt to take you away with him?"

Esmira shrank back, face lowered, shaking her head repeatedly. "No, my Lord, no!"

Swift as a striking snake, he grabbed her firmly by the hair. With his free hand, he pulled her head back hard and leaned in close, close enough to breathe in her sweet gasps, breath to final breath.

"Yes," he said.

And raising his sword, he drew its gleaming razor-sharp edge across the girl's throat.

Unclasping his hand, he let the blood-soaked girl fall to the stones where she gurgled and flopped weakly. Stepping over her, he pointed the quivering tip of his bloodied sword at Kuda and screamed, "Kill him!"

Blades bared, the bodyguards, Orkhon's all, ran toward the interloper. But Kuda was no longer there. In his place stood a beast, resurrected from out of some fevered nightmare by the sight of the slaughtered girl. Red eyes now burned out of a savage, primeval face that had lost all human expression.

He twisted aside to let a blade slip past him, then reached over his shoulder to yank his saber from its sheath. In the same, swift movement, he swept it over and down to sever the attacker's hand at the wrist. Blood hosed from the stump as the man staggered to a halt. A backhand slash sent his head cartwheeling into the air. Then the others were upon him, and the beast hewed right and left.

†

Stul stared for a moment at the broad empty stairway that had been so suddenly abandoned by the guards. Then, shrugging, he hefted the heavy bag he was carrying over his shoulder and started up the steps. As he neared the top, he could hear the clash and scrape of steel. He had to skip quickly aside when a headless body hurtled down the steps, spurting blood.

†

A sword whipped out for his throat. Kuda battered it aside and, with a full-throated berserker bellow, drove his blade down to split the man from shoulder to stomach. Kicking the corpse off his blade, he struck out again, but his saber sliced through empty air. The Orkhons were backing away, staring fearfully at something over his shoulder. Kuda snarled and stood panting, his features frozen in a rictus of fury. Feeling a presence, a trace of uneasiness showed in his face. Blinking away the last red haze of the berserker rage, he slowly turned.

The demon was ten paces away, standing perfectly still. A ten-foot tall spindly figure, slightly stooped and quite motionless. It wore an all-enveloping garment that covered it from high-domed head to ankles, the grey cloth pierced only by a pair of holes for the hands and a narrow slit for vision. The vision-slit was itself covered by a veil of fine-netting, so that nothing of the creature's face could be seen. The dragon keeper had clothed itself in the stuff of ancient nightmares, from times even before humans came down out of the trees. Horror washed over Kuda in sickening waves. His muscles locked in a terrifying paralysis.

The keeper raised one claw-like, three-fingered hand to pull aside the veil. An eye, like an enormous shelled egg, rolled to meet Kuda's petrified gaze. It was a large, rheumy eye, with the slightly opaque blue cast of age, giving it a look of great wisdom and infinite sorrow. That sorrow was contagious. It engulfed Kuda in a black wave and weighed down his soul, transforming his vital predatory passion to a devastating sadness and mourning for his life, the life that was about to end. The unblinking eye looked deep into his own. It seemed to pierce his very soul, mourning for him as he mourned for himself. The Northman did not realize that a great malevolence was burrowing into his brain, bending and reshaping reality. He only knew that the sorrow within him was so insupportable, he welcomed the black oblivion of death.

Unnoticed by him, his saber clattered to the paving. It was as though he had left his own body and hovered just above it, looking down upon himself, watching both the man and the demon. There was death in them, and death all about them. The tragedy engrossed him and robbed him of his will and power of movement. His consciousness was torn from him and hurled across unimaginable distances beyond time and space, to witness a planet screaming beneath a dying sun. Death, all was death.

†

Quickening his pace, Stul arrived at the top of the steps, where he was almost bowled over by a rush of Orkhon bodyguards. They bounded past him, leaping down the stairs in panicked flight. "Women!" he shouted after them, sneeringly. "One lone barbarian and you shit your pants!"

210

He made an obscene gesture at their backs before climbing the final step, where a terrible, milky-clouded eye swung onto him and he voided his bowels. He came to an abrupt halt, unable to take another step. A strange prickling sensation came over him, paralyzing him from head to toe. Rooted to the spot, he was unable to take his eyes off the tall, lanky nightmarish creature before him.

"Mercy!" Stul began whimpering. He half crouched, not daring to look. The cloth bag fell from his hands and the star-stone rolled out onto the paving.

The Khan's face lit with a slow, deep joy when he recognized the true star-stone. Slamming his sword back into its scabbard, he stooped down to retrieve it. But before his hands could close upon the celestial rock, it lifted into the air. The final Gods tear floated motionlessly in front of his face, pulsating with an inner fire until, across the pyramids summit, the dragon keeper extended one corpse-white arm and beckoned. Swift as a falcon, the glowing meteorite flew to its alien master.

When that fathomless gaze shifted from him, Kuda's body shook and spasmed. His eyes bulged out of their sockets and his mouth gaped. He uttered a chilling gasp before he slumped heavily forward.

The Gods tear slowed to settle gently onto the dragon keepers outstretched and waiting hands. As soon as it had done so, the alien being levered itself around and scurried back into the temple as fast as its strange angular limbs could carry it.

"Wait!" The Khan cried piteously, and set off after the dragon keeper. As he ran past Kuda's sprawled form, a hand shot out and tripped him. The Great Khan went down in a clatter of expensive mail.

Kuda struggled to his feet to stand on shaky legs. "You wait," he snarled and bent to retrieve his saber.

The Kuruk leader heaved himself to his feet, brushed his errant scalp-lock out of his eyes, and wordlessly shed his cloak. Curling thick fingers around the bejeweled hilt of his sword, he slowly eased the great blade from its scabbard. "I do not have time for this," he hissed, spittle flying from his lips.

Kuda eyed the Khan's crimsoned blade and rasped, "It won't take long."

He was the Khan but he was also a grim-faced, hard-eyed, battle-forged warrior. He bellowed death at Kuda as he sprang and lunged with lightning speed. Kuda parried, grunting with the effort it took to deflect the thrust. The Khan cut towards his head. Kuda ducked, only to receive a hard kick in the chest that sent him staggering backwards. The Khan spun away and darted into the temple. Kuda sprinted after him. The steppe-riders' leader whirled again, swung low and chopped at his legs. Jumping over the scything blade, he came down behind the stroke and hacked at the man's exposed back. The Khan shrieked and reeled away, his excellent mail saving him from a mortal wound. Once again, he ran, this time down the worn steps leading back into the Ziggurat. Kuda plunged after him, his reason lost in a haze of fury and revenge.

He hit the bottom of the stairs and sprinted flat out along the darkened tunnel, his labored breathing and heavy footfalls echoing off the stone walls. By the familiar sinister light that illuminated the pyramids interior, Kuda saw the Khan burst out of the tunnel mouth. Without hesitating, the armored man clattered across the metal gangplank, which led to the tower's now firmly shut door. Slamming up against the tower's side, the Khan desperately hammered his sword hilt against the metal.

"The dragon! The dragon!" he wailed bitterly. "I must ascend. It is my destiny!"

TEARS OF THE GODS

Pulling himself back from a full run, Kuda advanced out over the long drop and onto the perilously fragile bridge that shivered and swayed with each step he took.

The Khan whipped around to fix him with burning fanatical eyes. "You ignorant, mindless savage! You have no idea what you have done."

With an inhuman cry, the crazed man rushed at Kuda. They met and parried, their blades locked and straining against each other. Kuda gave a pace, and another, then another as the Khan pressed him with a strength born of madness. The barbarian twisted aside suddenly and the Khan staggered forward, off balance, rolling his head to avoid a cut that sliced at his face. Ready for the reverse, Kuda blocked it. Steel rang on steel. There was a tremendous eruption and the narrow gantry shook violently, forcing both men to disengage and concentrate on keeping their footing. A furnace blast of heat engulfed them. Kuda snatched a glance over the bridge's low guard rail. Far below them, the base of the tower had exploded into flames. A roiling grey-white plume of smoke began rolling up the tower's side.A tingle at the base of his neck caused him to twist aside. The Khan's heavy blade hammered into the rail where his head had been. Pivoting swiftly, Kuda backswung a blow that would have disemboweled a yak. The Khan leapt back, avoiding the blow by a hair's breadth just as the boiling cloud of smoke reached them and obscured everything. Suddenly, the entire pyramid shuddered under a tremendous jolt. The smoke cleared and Kuda found himself transfixed by a sight that had him doubting his senses. It took him a moment to register what he was seeing. The entire tower was moving, rising up into the air before his very eyes. The gangway, caught up against the tower's irresistible movement, buckled and tilted, throwing the two combatants off their feet. Kuda slammed up against the guard rail with an impact that knocked the breath from him. His saber went flying from his hand. A rasping, scraping noise made him look up to see the Khan, in his heavy mail coat, sliding helplessly down the smooth, slanting metal toward the edge of the bridge. Flailing with both hands, the Kuruk leader managed to grasp an iron stanchion that stopped him abruptly, swinging him around, and leaving him hanging by one hand over the sucking void.

There was a noise like that of a great boulder set in motion. An all-consuming rumbling that shook the bones. All around, the Ziggurat's soaring walls were vibrating, shifting, as if about to collapse. Kuda shook himself and began scrambling along the gantry that creaked and swayed alarmingly until he was staring down into the Khan's face. A face that no longer showed any trace of madness. With the heavy mail armor pulling at him and his legs kicking empty air, the Khan stared back, his eyes filled with the realization of death.

"Help me," he rasped.

"I was trying to," grated Kuda. "You should have given me the girl."

The Khan nodded, as though admitting his mistake, and said, almost to himself, "Destiny is all." And let go.

Kuda watched his body plummet straight down to be swallowed up by a roaring sea of flame.

Streamers of fire reached up towards Kuda as he frantically scrambled back along the shaking metal bridge. The ascending tower, its speed increasing, battered through the top of the pyramid's structure. Gargantuan blocks of masonry began falling all around like autumn leaves. One of the blocks smashed into the flimsy gantry, tearing it away. Kuda launched himself into space as hard as he could. He flew through the air over a holocaust of fire, then he was dropping. The impetus gone from his leap and he threw his hands out looking for something to grip, some edge, anything. His fingertips brushed stone and he managed to cling on, arresting his fall so that his body swung down to slam into the pyramid wall. Lifting his eyes, he saw the archway above him; he was hanging from the lip of the tunnel. Straining and heaving, he swung with his legs. The fire lashed at him until the great muscles of his chest and arms locked in an iron convulsion and he managed to pull himself up, rolling over the lip, mere seconds before a sheet of flame seared across the tunnel's open mouth. Staggering to his feet, he ran down the trembling stone pipe with a tumbling mass of fire at his heels. Racing up the steps, he plunged through the collapsing temple just ahead of an all-consuming explosion that turned everything into an inferno. He left the ground as a wave of burnt air hit him from behind and blasted him off his feet. Landing hard on his shoulder, he rolled across the paving until he dropped off the edge of the Ziggurat to tumble down the quaking steps. Gaining his feet on the rocking masonry, he half fell, half ran, down the side of the disintegrating structure amidst an avalanche of dust and rubble, expecting to be crushed to death at any second. He could see people running, fleeing from the cataclysm taking place before them. All around the crater's rim, vast columns of fire seared across the steppe, turning night into day.

Reaching level ground, he ran until the roar no longer seemed to pursue him, until his legs gave way and he fell onto his back and looked up. His eyes widened at what he saw and he felt his sanity slipping away from him. A thundering roar echoed across the world as he witnessed the slim tower rising majestically from the crumbling Ziggurat. It seemed to hang for a moment before a perfect sphere of white fire blossomed like a miniature sun at its base. Moving at incredible speed, it soared straight up into the night sky. From somewhere underground came a series of rumbling explosions, the earth shook and the remains of the pyramid teetered and finally collapsed under its own weight. The dragon had risen.

†

In the brooding dawn, Kuda the barbarian sat atop the crater's escarpment and stared into the distance. The sun marched slowly up the sky as he sat there, watching the morning move on, his thoughts empty, the pain across his body slowly easing from a strident throbbing to a dull ache. He kept waiting for the moment to come, for some fraction of understanding to strike him, for some new insight to rise from the course he had taken. But there was nothing, only a faint, enduring sorrow. Behind him, a column of smoke writhed and twisted into the morning sky. It was issuing from a smaller, deeper and newer crater within the larger older crater. He was alone, the place was deserted, the people had scattered in terror. From his vantage point, he could still see some of them running away. Tiny dots upon the grassland that stretched to the limits of his vision in every direction. He was about to turn away when something caught his attention. Peering into the misty, half-light that still obscured the plain, he could just make out a wiry figure. The wiry figure of a short man. There was something so familiar about the half stumbling, half running figure that Kuda felt a savage elation flare in his chest. Plucking the hunting knife from his boot, he set off down the steep slope. He had one final oath to discharge.

THE END

Printed in Great Britain
by Amazon